# *Hart's* TAVERN

Elaine Kiesling Whitehouse

To Pat and Don-
Best wishes
Elaine Whitehouse

**HART'S TAVERN**



*iUniverse books may be ordered through booksellers or by contacting:*

*iUniverse LLC*
*1663 Liberty Drive*
*Bloomington, IN 47403*
*www.iuniverse.com*
*1-800-Authors (1-800-288-4677)*



*ISBN: 978-1-4917-4026-2 (sc)*
*ISBN: 978-1-4917-4027-9 (e)*

*Printed in the United States of America.*

*iUniverse rev. date: 08/13/2014*

*Dedicated to all Patriots,*
*young and old.*

# Foreword

A stone marker stands on the site of what is believed to be the actual Hart's Tavern on Montauk Highway in Patchogue, Long Island. It reads, *Hart's Tavern, visited by George Washington, 1790.* However, the tavern may not have existed at all. Patchogue historian Hans Henke tells a different story.

Two boys were selling sweet potatoes by the side of the road. George Washington asked, "May I have a potato?" Then he asked their names.

"Masters Hart," they said.

Washington replied, "I am happy that I dined at Hart's Tavern."

# Chapter One

Let us step back in time to 1775, when the Redcoats filled the countryside of the colony of New York, causing fear and uncertainty among the colonists, slaves and Native Americans who lived there. Walk along a dirt road with the horses and carts, peddlers and travelers on their way to the town of New Kensington. Some of these travelers will stop at a small inn beside a pond where ducks and swans swim peacefully and the tips of a willow tree's branches brush the water as they sway in the breeze.

Look carefully. Near the weeping willow you will see a 14-year-old girl. Her unruly chestnut brown hair is tucked under a mobcap, but many curls escape. She is wearing a long brown dress, covered with an apron that used to be white but is now stained with streaks of deep blue-purple. She stands over a deep cauldron held in place over a low burning fire by an iron pole resting on crisscrossed posts. She is stirring the contents with a large stick.

The girl is Hannah Wainwright Hart, daughter of Peter Hart, owner of Hart's Tavern on the south shore of Long Island.

Hannah lifts her eyes skyward, squinting in the bright sunlight, cheered by the brilliant blue, cloudless sky. She hums a tune, to make the work seem easier. Perhaps she will see her friend Jeremy tonight. Perhaps he will stop at the inn for a glass of ale, and smile and wink at her as he sometimes does.

Hannah wipes the sweat from her brow with the back of her hand as she pounds the long stick up and down in the cauldron. It is hot and heavy work on such a warm day; her arms and back feel the strain. Steam rises from the purple-blue froth bubbling up from the bottom of the pot.

Round and round she stirs the thick, heavy wool. The indigo blue is a rare color. She will use it to dye the wool she has spun and sell it in the market. Perhaps she will save enough of the wool to make a shawl – no, two shawls – one to keep and one to give to her teacher, Miss White.

Nearby on the clothesline white linens billow in the breeze like the sails of the ships that sail off the barrier beach. Yes, Monday was always laundry day. There was no getting around it, and one might as well make the best of it.

The clothesline and dye pot stand behind her father's inn. Nearby are carefully cultivated rows of hops, tied neatly to stakes, almost ready to be harvested to make ale. Also nearby is the old, Dutch oven where Hannah bakes bread nearly every day. She also bakes pies and cakes every week to serve the guests, as well as jelly tarts and raisin scones. The aroma was delicious.

Hannah was happy. Yes, she had lots of hard work to do, and yes, life would have been better if her mother had lived, but she had her father and her older brother Thomas. Thomas was a wonderful brother. He showed her how to do things and protected her from people and events that might otherwise have made her life more difficult. But Thomas had left New Kensington to go to Boston. She missed him so! Why did he have to leave the inn, and her father? Why couldn't everything just stay the way it was? Why all this talk of liberty and war?

Suddenly Hannah's thoughts were interrupted. Out of the corner of her eye she caught a flash of steel and scarlet. She thought again that her wish for peace was hopeless, because the enemy was all around, all the time.

She did not know how many British troops were close, but she knew they would take all her cakes and pies and bread. They might even force themselves into the inn and demand to remain there, drinking all her father's ale and eating all their food. A sense of dread began to overtake her, rising like some black shroud from the soles of her feet to the top of her head. The sky no longer seemed so blue.

What could she do? She quickly wiped her hands on her apron, took a ladle and dipped it into the dye pot. She poured the ladle of dye into the bowl of flour on the table, and just as the British officers came into full sight she began to knead her dough.

"Good heavens!" said an officer. "Is that the way you mix your bread?"

"Aye, your honor, 'tis a bit weevily this year. Then she sneezed loudly over the dough, wiped her hand under her nose, and continued with her kneading. But, Sir, what difference does it make?"

"What difference! Why it makes a pile of difference to me!" snorted the officer. The others went away, shaking their heads and muttering, "The filthy, damnable rebels. Even their bread is dirty."

Hannah waited for a long while, continually kneading the blue-grey dough, until her hands were quite discolored with it. When she was sure the soldiers were gone she took the dough to the trash pile and buried it under the leaves. Then she washed her hands in the water bucket and made her way to the Dutch oven.

She opened the oven door and gathered up the fragrant bread, pies and cakes. These she would bring to the kitchen of the inn. She had made a special strawberry tart for Jeremy with the last of the strawberry jam, for she knew that was his favorite.

"There is more than one way to mix your dough," she said with a wry grin. Perhaps her blue bread would keep the British soldiers away for a bit longer. Perhaps her sneeze would keep them away from the inn.

# Chapter Two

The sign outside the inn had a red heart painted inside a pentagram under the name Hart's Tavern. The logo was an instantly recognizable symbol of the well-known Hart family business – an inn where people from town could enjoy a meal and conversation, or, if they had traveled a long distance, could comfortably spend the night.

The tavern was originally a small, wood structure built around 1650 by Ezekiel Redmond Hart, Hannah's great grandfather. Over the years, additions had been built so that now, in 1775, the inn was a three-story building with a barn and large kitchen at the back. There was also an attic with a gabled window. Hannah, her father and her brother, Thomas, had rooms on the first floor behind the dining room and bar. Evie, their slave, slept in a tiny room near the kitchen pantry. Upstairs there were five rooms where guests stayed.

Hart's Tavern was a small establishment, but it was well known for serving good food and having clean beds. Weary travelers, including merchants from New York en route to the easternmost reaches of Long Island, were their main customers, but occasionally a hunter or a traveling clergyman would stay.

When you entered the inn you would see on the left side of the doorway a rack containing clay pipes. Visitors could rent a pipe for the evening, but they had to bring their own tobacco.

On the other side of the doorway, a broadside was tacked to the wall, describing the news of New Kensington and listing advertisements and notices. Jeremy Moore, the print shop apprentice, would bring the latest broadsheet whenever he stopped at the inn.

When Hannah was little, before her mother died, the inn was a happy place. Sometimes a fiddler would play and people would dance. Once, a traveling magician put on a show. Hannah remembered jumping up and down and clapping her hands as the magician pulled a dove from his hat. But when her mother died, it seemed that some of the joy left Hart's Tavern.

Now meetings were held there, where a group of villagers and Hannah's father's friends would sit around the big oak table and discuss politics or the latest happenings in town. Sometimes her father would walk to the barn with a person Hannah did not recognize, or go down the narrow stairs into the ale cellar. Hannah suspected that these meetings were secret, having something to do with the Sons of Liberty, and all the talk of war.

Somehow, without her mother and with Thomas gone to Boston, Hannah, her father, and Evie managed to keep the inn going. It was hard work, cleaning the rooms, cooking and baking for the guests and themselves, growing hops to brew the ale, spinning, weaving, sewing . . . Hannah felt she did not have a moment to herself. But she still made time to go to school. Each morning, from seven until ten she went to the one- room schoolhouse, where she and six or seven other pupils met with their teacher, Miss Violet White, to learn history and geography, reading and arithmetic.

Hannah loved school, especially since Miss White had become their teacher at the start of the term. Hannah was grateful that she could go in the mornings most days, except, of course, for the weekends when she went to church. The Bible was the only book the students had to read, but Miss White told them other stories, about ancient Greece and Rome, Egypt and the pyramids. She described the latest fashions of France, and what the ladies of the court in London were wearing. It all sounded so wonderful to Hannah.

On the morning after her encounter with the British officers Hannah could not wait to get to school to tell Miss White what had happened. Only five students were present this day – Adeline Squires, the Jewell twins, and another lad from a neighboring farm. Hannah slid into her seat before any of the others. She observed Miss White, who sat waiting for her students on a high stool in front of the room, near the potbellied stove. The sun streamed in the windows, creating a golden glow of early autumn light.

Hannah admired the way the light shone on Miss White's lovely russet-colored hair. It was almost too beautiful to show off, yet Miss White did not cover it with a cap. Her dove-gray dress did not hide her feminine figure, either, and her straight, white smile was a rare sight among the colonists. How did she end up here, in New Kensington? Hannah wondered. Why she had left England, with its all sophistication – the art, the music?

Hannah said, "Miss White, I saw the soldiers near the inn yesterday. I am afraid they will try to force their way into our home." She hesitated for a moment, and then asked somewhat boldly, "Why did you leave England and come here?"

Miss White tucked her neat little boots onto the rung of her teacher's stool and said, "I came here to see the New World. I want to live a life of adventure. I want to see as much of the world as possible, and enjoy everything. When I have seen enough here, I will move on. I hope to visit India one day."

Hannah was fascinated with the idea of a life of adventure, of traveling around the world, a woman alone . . . Then with a shiver she realized that what Miss White said was close to blasphemy. Hannah knew the church taught that people were to suffer here on earth, and that their duty was to serve God and to live simply. A Christian's reward was a place in heaven in the afterlife. As far as Hannah knew, the Bible said nothing about seeking a life of adventure.

Hannah wondered what Miss White would do if the British took over New Kensington. Would she try to go back to England? Was she a Loyalist? Hannah did not know. At any rate, no one cared about a woman's political views. But somehow Miss White was different. Hannah suspected that she was a Patriot.

# Chapter Three

New Kensington consisted of a Main Street with a few shops, the church, and the Town Hall. Hart's Tavern was a good three miles down the road, and Melancholy Hollow was well beyond that. The Great Bay, with its miles of marshlands lay to the south. Separating the bay from the ocean, about four miles out, was the Barrier Island.

Reed grass as tall as a man grew alongside the marsh. Here there were nests of ducks, black skimmers, terns and kingfishers. Black and orange ladybugs, monarch butterflies and bright peacock-blue dragonflies darted among the reeds. Occasionally one of them would stray from the reeds and alight on a young woman's basket.

The young woman was Evie, slave of Peter Hart. On this golden September day she walked barefooted on the marsh. She was pressing her feet into the thick, gooey black mud in what looked like a curious dance, but she was actually hunting for the fat eels that lived beneath the shallow water. Out popped a head and Evie quickly scooped it up, its glistening black body writhing and twisting like a snake. Evie thrust it in her basket and closed the lid. She repeated this action until her basket was full of squirming eels, ready to be baked into pies or jellied or pickled for future use. The basket grew heavy, and Evie was getting tired. She gathered her skirts with her free hand and made her way through the reeds towards the road. She stopped when she saw a flash of color. Quietly setting down her basket, she stood motionless. Three Redcoats stood talking, no more than ten feet away. She could not hear what they were saying, but she sensed a restlessness about them. She feared these men and their swords.

Then a wave of claustrophobia came over her and she suddenly felt weak in the knees. There was something about these soldiers that reminded her of the slave dealers. Her hand moved involuntarily to her left thigh, where she had felt the sting of their whip when she was just a small girl, and where a thick scar was hidden under her plain skirt. She waited there, motionless, trying not to breathe, until at last the Redcoats moved on down the road towards town. Evie waited still longer, until she was sure they were out of sight.

Then she hurried in the opposite direction, along the path that ran alongside the marsh to Melancholy Hollow, her eel basket bumping against her leg, until she came to the place where the land suddenly rose slightly to reveal a thicket of shrubs and a stand of tall birch trees. She leaned against one of them to catch her breath. This was a good place to stop and rest, just for a moment, out of sight and out of the wind.

Evie noticed a small outcropping of stones under the birch trees. She had seen it before, but had never really looked at the stones. Today she realized they were not part of the natural landscape, but had been placed there by someone. They were arranged in an overlapping circular pattern. The stones must be a marker, she thought, perhaps a grave. A shiver ran through her thin body. The sun was getting low, the air chill.

Again Evie thought of the Redcoats. Where were they staying? Maybe they were on their way to Hart's Tavern right now, she thought. She realized she must tell Miss Hannah. She gathered up her skirts and basket and quickly made her way back to the inn.

# Chapter Four

Before dusk Hannah left the dye pot to cool and hung the dyed wool on two clotheslines near the hops garden. When she was finished she noticed that Tinker, one of the cats who lived at the Tavern and earned his keep by scaring away the mice, had a suspiciously blue tint to his normally white fur. Hannah scooped him up with a laugh and carried him to her room.

Soon it would be time for Hannah to serve dinner to the Inn's guests. Evie was already busy preparing the food in the kitchen, where a large pot of mutton stew simmered over the fire. Kegs of ale and pitchers of lemonade were ready. The bread that Hannah had baked was still warm and fragrant, as were the apple and peach pies. Hannah had just enough time to change her apron, wash her face and comb her hair. She would not have time to write to Thomas until later, when she was in bed, a candle lighting her dim room sufficiently for her to put her quill upon paper.

Once in her room, Hannah poured water from a pitcher into the china washbowl that sat on a small chest of drawers. She picked up a bar of lye soap from the soap dish and scrubbed her hands. Then she peered into the tiny looking glass that hung on the wall. Her face was streaked faintly with indigo. Would she ever be as attractive as Miss White, she wondered, as she scrubbed away the traces of dye. She wrinkled her freckled nose and blinked her blue eyes. She opened her mouth and inspected her back teeth, then grimaced so that all her front teeth showed. The teeth looked good, she thought, straight and white and her eyes were bright and pretty enough. Her chestnut brown hair was often a tangle of thick curls, but she kept them under control, most of the time anyway, with her mobcap. She washed and dried her face, paying special attention to the streaks of dye. With a final glance in the mirror she decided she probably never would be as beautiful as Miss White, but she was not bad looking either. After all, many a young man had pinched her on the cheek when she served them, and told her what a fine-looking little wench she was, until her father appeared and frowned at them.

Hannah tucked a stray curl under her cap as she entered the dining area. A few men were seated at the bar, pints of frothy ale in front of them. Hannah kept her head down. While she was pleasant and polite with everyone, she did not like fraternizing with strangers, and her father did not approve of her conversing at length with the patrons.

Few women stayed at the inn, although tonight a fat matron sat at a side table with a shorter, rather thin looking man whom Hannah supposed was her husband. The woman raised her arm to signal Hannah to the table.

"Is mutton stew the only thing you are serving this evening?" she asked with a frown. "I do not like the taste of mutton stew."

"I am sorry, ma'am, but mutton stew is the main course for the day. I assure you it is most delicious and savory, made with fresh herbs I picked myself this morning."

The woman's lower lip stuck out, in a very odd manner, thought Hannah, who suddenly realized she had been staring. "Have you nothing else?" demanded the woman.

"I can see if there is any jellied eel left from our midday meal, or perhaps some fresh tripe. Would that suit you better?" Hannah tried to keep her voice even. This woman had no idea how hard she and her father and Evie worked to provide three good meals each day for the guests.

The woman sighed as if in misery while her husband looked on with discomfort. "Surely the mutton stew will do us fine," he said, but his voice was raised at the end of his statement as if he were posing a question. He was a small man, in comparison to his wife. His powdered wig was slightly askew. Hannah noticed that he adjusted it frequently. She wondered if it itched.

The woman harrumphed and flung her foxtail around her shoulders. "I suppose it will have to do," she said unpleasantly.

Hannah turned to get away when the door opened with a bang. There stood Jeremy, his large frame filling the doorway, a wide grin on his face. His gaze rested on Hannah for a moment. Then he gestured for her to join him at the bar.

"I have something for you," he said with a wink. Reaching into his coat pocket he drew out a fold of paper that looked like a letter. Hannah stood at his elbow while he placed the paper on the bar and opened it carefully. It was not a letter at all. Within its folds were four little seeds.

"These are orange pips," Jeremy told Hannah. A traveler gave me an orange in payment for placing an advertisement. I thought t'would be something if you could get them to grow, or at least one of them. You are a clever girl with plants."

Hannah placed the packet of seeds in her apron pocket, and smiled with delight. She had eaten an orange once. She got one last year for Christmas. It was, perhaps, the most delicious thing she had ever tasted. Imagine if she could grow a whole tree full of them!

"I expect these seeds are strangers to the cold and winds of these parts," she said. "I expect they wouldn't grow outside."

"I expect you are right," said Jeremy, with another wink. "But maybe you can grow them indoors. Maybe your teacher can tell you what they need."

"Thank you, Jeremy. This is a fine gift! I promise that if I can make them grow you will have plenty of oranges!"

She was unaware of the others at the bar who had witnessed their conversation, and who now broke out into a little applause. She felt her face grow hot. Bobbing a curtsey she retreated to her small room. She couldn't wait to figure out a way to plant the seeds and help them grow.

That night she dipped a new quill into her inkbottle and gently wiped its tip. Then she wrote,

*Dear Thomas,*

*Father and I are managing all right, and the inn is full most nights. Father shot several wild turkeys so we'll be having those for dinner the next few weeks. The sheep are sheared and I have dyed the wool a deep indigo from dye that I obtained from the market. A case of it was brought up from Virginia on a ship called Valkyrie. I happened to be at the market when the crates were opened.*

*We do miss you, dear Thomas. Jeremy at the news office asks after you as well as others in town. He gave me a splendid gift this evening! Four orange pips that I intend to make grow so that everyone who comes to Hart's Tavern can enjoy oranges! I must ask Miss White, my new teacher, how to grow them. She is well traveled and knowledgeable about the most extraordinary things. She is also kind and pretty, holding no comparison to the former schoolmaster, Mr. Dowd.*

*Miss White says war is imminent, that there is no getting around it. This frightens me, dear brother, with you being in Boston. I wish you would come home to New Kensington. I have seen three British soldiers who have made nuisances of themselves, but nothing else. I tricked them when they would have stolen the bread I was making. I shall tell you about that when I see you. Muffin had a litter of kittens, most of them white. Father is well. Please write soon.*

*Your loving sister,*
*Hannah Wainwright Hart*

Hannah put down her quill beside the little glass inkbottle, and was about to replace its brass top. Then she changed her mind and picked up the feather again and dipped its tip into the ink. She took out another sheet of paper from her paper box. Her writing paper was precious, so she used it only for important things, like writing letters to Thomas. At school she used a hornbook for writing, not paper. But just now, as she finished her letter, she felt she needed to write something important for herself. Picking up the quill, she wrote:

*What Shall I be?*

*I am fourteen years old. In two years I should seek a husband and perhaps have a child. Where shall I live? Shall I remain at Hart's Tavern? Who will be my husband? Will he be a farmer? A merchant? Could it be Jeremy?"*

*"On the other hand, would I prefer to live a life of adventure, like Miss White? Could I travel to exotic places? Would I meet famous people, like Benjamin Franklin?*

*These things I wonder.*

*September 26, 1775*

Hannah decided she would wait a year and see how she felt about these questions. Also in a year maybe one or more of the orange pips would have started to grow into trees! In the corner of the paper she wrote,

*"To be opened on September 26, 1776."*

When the ink was dry she folded the paper, and put it in the bottom of her letterbox.

# Chapter Five

Mr. and Mrs. Hewitt left the inn two days later. Hannah could not say she was sorry to see them leave, although having a woman guest had been an unusual occurrence. Mrs. Hewitt was often disagreeable. Hannah smiled when she thought of how Mr. Hewitt, who cowered from his wife, secretly drank ale at the bar when she was not looking.

On the afternoon of the day before the Hewitts left the inn, Hannah and Mrs. Hewitt were walking near the hops garden, where the golden light of the low sun filtered through the deep green leaves.

"What in the world are these?" asked Mrs. Hewitt, pointing to the little green cones that grew on the vines like grapes.

"Hops, Mrs. Hewitt. "It is from hops that we make our own ale, along with some other ingredients."

"Such as?" she demanded.

"Well, molasses and yeast," said Hannah, "and flavorings. Some of them are Hart's Tavern's special secret ingredients."

"Well I never!" harrumphed Mrs. Hewitt. Then to change the subject, she said, "I must say you have a lot of goldenrod growing wild around here!" She extended her chubby arm in a sweeping motion to indicate the swath of goldenrod growing alongside the tended garden.

"Indeed, we do," replied Hannah. "I like its cheerful color, don't you?" Hannah proceeded to show Mrs. Hewitt the flower garden, which was fairly well spent except for a few zinnias. She pointed out the path beside the stream that led to the meadow and beyond, and finally to the Great Bay. They walked along the rough path for a while, without saying a word.

"Would you like to continue, Mrs. Hewitt?" asked Hannah, when she noticed that Mrs. Hewitt had become quite red in the face.

"No, no thank you," she said. "I think I've done enough walking for one day." She pulled a folding fan out of her cummerbund and began to fan herself vigorously.

Suddenly in the distance two men on horseback appeared. Hannah pointed to them. "Redcoats," she said.

"Are many of them here?" asked Mrs. Hewitt.

"Not so many, at least not yet," replied Hannah. "Miss White said she expects more will arrive if the fighting comes to New York."

They turned to slowly make their way back to the inn. "They should go back where they came from!" Mrs. Hewitt declared. "The only reason they are here is so the King can get money to pay for the Seven Years' war that drained the British treasury. Now he wants us to pay!"

"Can we not pay?" asked Hannah naively.

Once again Mrs. Hewitt harrumphed. Hannah expected her to gesture the way she did when she tossed her fox furs around her shoulders, but it was warm today, and Mrs. Hewitt was not wearing them.

Instead, she raised her fat fist in the air and declared, "It is taxation without representation, and I'll not pay it!"

It was the first time Hannah had heard this fateful expression. Mrs. Hewitt stomped up the path to the inn, and soon the pair reached the door to the tavern. Mrs. Hewitt pushed it open, and then stood there with her hands on her hips. Mr. Hewitt sat at the bar, a large tankard of ale in front of him, talking and laughing with one of the other men who sat there. But his smile faded rapidly when he saw who stood in the doorway. With the sun behind her, his wife looked like a buffalo in the sunset.

"Phineas Hewitt! Whatever are you doing, drinking ale in the afternoon!"

Hannah put her hand over her mouth to hide her smile and hurried to her room, leaving the Hewitts to their argument. They were silent that evening at dinner, and they left the inn the next morning. Hannah thought that would be the last she saw of them.

But three weeks later, the pair rolled up to the inn in a stagecoach. They had a trunk between them and a few suitcases. Hannah bade them come in and sit while she hurried to get her father, who was working in the barn.

Hannah and her father stood dumbfounded while Mrs. Hewitt sat at one of the tables and wept loudly while Mr. Hewitt adjusted his wig with embarrassment.

"We've lost our home!" she wailed. "The Redcoats have taken it over, as well as the homes of our friends and neighbors. They took all our food, all our money. We had no place else to go, so we came here." She put her head on her arms and sobbed, while Mr. Hewitt patted her shoulder and regarded Hannah and her father apologetically.

He cleared his throat. "We were wondering," he said hesitatingly. "We were wondering if we might stay here a while? We know you could use some help, being without a wife and all. We'd help you manage. We would not expect any pay, of course, if you could just give us a room until we can get our home back."

Without a moment's hesitation, Peter Hart said, "Of course you can stay! Evie, Prepare the big room for the Hewitts."

And that is how the Hewitts came to stay at Hart's Tavern.

# Chapter Six

One bright afternoon, as Hannah made her way down Main Street, she passed the stocks and whipping post located in the town square in the middle of the village. She was glad they were seldom used. New Kensington was a peaceful place. The last time she remembered anyone in the stocks was when Simon Billings, age sixteen, was caught stealing a pig from Mr. Barrow's livestock barn at the edge of town. The town magistrate ruled that Simon had to spend four hours in the stocks, return the pig, and shovel manure for Mr. Barrow for several weeks. The whole incident was treated somewhat as a joke, with Simon laughing along with everyone for a while, until standing in the stocks grew tedious. Public whippings, on the other hand, were rare. Hannah shuddered at the thought. She had heard the last time one occurred was when an escaped slave was caught and whipped. Hannah was glad she had not seen this happen.

Also near the Town Square was the office of the *New Kensington Chronicle*, the weekly newspaper run by Hiram McDowell and his apprentice, Jeremy Moore. Outside the office, pasted on the fence, was the weekly broadsheet that told about local events as well as what was happening in the world. Hannah stopped and read:

*A town meeting will be held to discuss the problem of horses running through the town at a fast pace to the dangerment of our citizens. Horses must now be kept tethered at all times. New places designated for such tethering will be discussed.*

And further down:

*The yearly Christmas market will offer fine baked goods, textiles, wines, and other specialty items at reasonable prices. Those wishing to participate should see Mistress Penelope Hyde.*

And finally, Hannah read:

*A smallpox epidemic has been rampant among the students at Yale College, causing the campus to close. There have been no cases in our area, but persons are advised to avoid contact with anyone carrying the disease.*

Not much good news, thought Hannah. No mention of the British officers who were in town. How many of them were here?

She walked up the steps and rapped lightly on the door of the news office before entering. The smell of paper and ink filled her nostrils. She liked the smells and sounds of the print shop. Not only was the *New Kensington Chronicle* printed here, but also all manner of pamphlets, legal forms, advertisements, deeds and broadsheets. Eleven years ago, when Hannah was only three, an odious tax known as the Stamp Tax was repealed when the colonists rioted against officers who tried to enforce the unpopular law. Mr. McDowell told Hannah that he was required to purchase stamps to put on all his publications. It was one more tax that made the colonists angry with the British and caused them to desire independence.

At the sound of Hannah's knock Jeremy Moore came out from the back of the shop, wiping his inky hands on a rough apron.

"Well, it is Hannah Hart," he said, smiling. "What can I do for you today?"

"My father would like to place a small advertisement in the next *Chronicle*," said Hannah. "He wants to sell a small plow that he rarely uses."

"I see. And what else does he wish to sell?" Jeremy left that question open. He knew that Hannah and her father worked hard to make ends meet at the inn.

"Nothing else, thank you," said Hannah. Then on impulse she said, "Our cat had a litter of kittens. I can give you one or two in a few weeks, to keep away the mice. I forgot to tell you the last time you were at the inn – when you gave me the orange pips. Thank you again."

"You're welcome!" Jeremy laughed heartily. "Now just what makes you think we have mice around here?" he asked.

Hannah was nonplussed. "Everyone has mice, especially as the weather grows colder." She sniffed, as if insulted. "I just thought I would ask. I'll not have my kittens be sent off to a place where they are not wanted."

"Well, I'll ask Mr. McDowell about the kittens." He paused for a moment, cleared his throat, then said, "And how have you been, Hannah?" His voice was more serious, the smile gone. Hannah wondered if he thought her dress looked shabby, or if he thought she was too thin. These thoughts made her feel heat come into her face.

"Thank you, Jeremy, I am well."

"The British soldiers are quartered in town, in rooms over the post office and boarding in some of the houses. I am wondering how you have avoided them at Hart's Tavern."

"My father has wondered the same thing," replied Hannah. "But we have no room. We have paying guests who have reserved rooms straight through the Christmas season. There would be no place to put the soldiers."

Jeremy shook his head. "Be careful. If they have orders from the king, your paying guests will be sent away and the soldiers will move in."

Hannah said nothing, but nodded her head. She wondered what would happen in New Kensington. She sensed there was something big going on, beyond the realm of this small village, beyond even Boston and Philadelphia. Somehow she knew that what was to come would cause enormous changes, but she could not say how. She felt it as a premonition. It was something she wanted to talk about with Miss White.

Hannah bid good-bye to Jeremy and proceeded down Main Street. Across from the print shop were several small markets. She passed the bakery, where delicious smells lingered in the air, and the leather goods merchant. She passed the fruit and vegetable stands, the fish monger and the butcher shop. At the far end of Main Street were the blacksmith's shop and the joiners, and at the cross street was Miss Fisk's dry goods store, which also housed the post office.

The church was located just beyond these buildings. It was a tidy, white structure, with a polished oak door and a small stained glass window over the altar. This window was the pride and joy of New Kensington. It was made in Rome, Italy, and had been brought to the town aboard a British ship by a family who had later died of typhoid fever. Some people said the window did not belong in a Protestant Church, where pride was looked upon as a sin. But Hannah loved this window. When her mind wandered during Reverend Windsor's long sermons she stared at its jeweled colors and wondered how it was made. Someone had drawn it first, she decided, then cut out pieces of glass to fit the drawing. The colored pieces of glass – crimson, indigo, amber, green and crystal – pictured Jesus, with his arms outstretched among flowers and trees. His gentle face melded into a design that caught the light when the sun was at a certain angle. Seeing the sun streaming through the stained glass window was one of the things she always looked forward to.

On Sundays Hannah often went to church with Adeline Squires and Adeline's family. Hannah's father usually stayed at the inn, to keep an eye on things. Work was generally forbidden on the Sabbath, but Peter Hart did not abide by these rules. He had the guests to take care of as well as the hops, the casks of ale in the cellar, his horses, a cow, and some goats and pigs, as well as his accounts. So Hannah put on her best dress and shawl and walked briskly into the village alone, heading for Adeline's house. Several people were out on Main Street, many of them couples who walked arm in arm, on that bright autumn day. They all waved to her, perhaps commenting to each other about what a shame it was for the thin, pretty, motherless girl to be walking through town alone.

Hannah and Adeline had been friends since they were little. Mrs. Squires and Hannah's mother, Clara Hart, sometimes sat together and sewed while the two girls played. When Hannah's mother died, Mrs. Squires had kindly continued to invite Hannah to come to the fine house where Adeline lived with her parents and baby sister. Mr. Squires was judge and magistrate for New Kensington. He was a Loyalist who would hear no talk of rebellion, although he did understand why the people were upset about the new taxes being imposed on them. He had engaged Peter Hart in many heated discussions on the subject of taxation.

Soon she was outside Adeline's house, knocking at the door with the big brass knocker in the shape of a lion's head. The brick house had two stories and four bedrooms. Dark green velvet drapes hung from the tall windows of the parlor. The furniture was polished, and fine oriental carpets covered the floors. The Squires family owned three slaves who maintained their large farm and this house. Hannah realized that Mr. and Mrs. Squires might be reluctant to allow Adeline to visit Hannah at the tavern, with the inn guests drinking ale, singing and even dancing at times. She understood perfectly. And yet sometimes she wished she could show Adeline the new litter of kittens and the gardens. She wished they could ride Badger and Honeycomb, galloping though the meadow at top speed. Adeline had recently stopped going to school, after Hannah had encountered the soldiers near the inn. Adeline's mother was teaching her at home instead.

Soon Adeline herself answered the door. She was a tall girl, fourteen years of age like Hannah, with long, dark hair curled in ringlets and brown eyes like buttons. Today she wore a yellow dress adorned with matching ribbons. A pang of envy pierced through Hannah, not only for Adeline's pretty dress but also for Adeline's mother, who stood in the doorway of the parlor. She was a lovely woman, with delicate hands and dark hair piled elegantly on her head. She reached for her bonnet and put it on, adjusting the ribbons and brim. Hannah felt lightheaded for a moment as a memory of her own mother, tying her bonnet, flashed through her mind. She tried to put aside painful thoughts like these, but sometimes they came unbidden, and their effect was like a sudden, unexpected blow. Hannah found herself gripping the stair rail to regain her composure.

# Chapter Seven

The next day Violet White was walking down Main Street toward the schoolhouse. She stopped to read the latest broadsheet posted on the big oak tree outside the print office when she saw two soldiers in the street. She overheard a bit of their conversation as the soldiers passed.

"I hear there's a schoolhouse nearby," said the one with light hair. "Might make a good encampment," said the dark-haired soldier. Violet frowned. It seemed more and more British soldiers were appearing in New Kensington every day. The colonies were run under a policy of "benign neglect," meaning that King George III of England had paid little notice of these colonies for years, but now that the king had run out of money, he demanded new taxes from the colonists and sent his soldiers to enforce his law.

Violet picked up her skirts and walked briskly towards the schoolhouse, ignoring the soldiers whom she sensed were watching her. She wondered how many students would come today. The boys' attendance, especially, had been dwindling, as more and more of them became busy with harvesting, and, she suspected, with meetings of the Sons of Liberty. Her best student was Hannah Hart. She'd been coming regularly, and was interested in everything.

Violet wrapped her wool shawl around her shoulders and followed a tree-lined path down a little hill leading to the meadow and the schoolhouse. The schoolhouse was a small structure, actually a barn that the men of the town had refurbished. They had also made plank benches and a few tables. The pride of the room was the cast iron pot bellied stove that kept the place warm in winter. In a few weeks the children would take turns tending the stove as well as cleaning up the room.

Violet passed Goody Garlicke's cottage on the hill, near where the path forked. To the east were Melancholy Hollow and the Great Bay; to the west, Hart's Tavern and the schoolhouse.

Today Violet carried with her a book she wanted to show Hannah and the other students. Books were scarce in the colonies, but Violet had several that she had brought with her from London. Her father had quite a library there.

Soon the schoolhouse came into view. Violet opened the door, dusted off her desk and neatly arranged a pile of papers. There were also a dozen hornbooks on which the children could practice their letters. The hornbooks were little paddles upon which a sheet of paper was pasted. On the paper were printed the Lord's Prayer and the letters of the alphabet. Atop the paper was a thin sheet of transparent cow's horn, which the children could write upon. Paper was scarce and expensive, and was never used to practice writing the alphabet.

A scuttling noise startled her. Another mouse! She must find a cat to keep them away. Perhaps the cat could live in the schoolhouse, a guard against the rats. Hannah loved animals. Perhaps she would help feed it and take care of it. But now the sound was louder, and Violet turned around to see a large, dark haired man standing in the doorway, dressed in a Redcoat with a sword at his side. He was one of the two soldiers she had seen on Main Street. She stood facing him.

"Can I help you?" she asked. Her gaze was level, her voice calm.

The soldier looked at her, then around the room, before he spoke. "You must be the school marm," he said, with a thin-lipped grin. He turned around, beckoning another soldier, the other one she had seen earlier, by the tree.

"T'would make a fine encampment, said the second soldier, but I don't see a kitchen. Perhaps the stove would do." The two men laughed loudly. Then he went on, "Perhaps the wench could do the cooking! Ah, but she's the school marm. Maybe she could teach us a thing or two."

The first soldier took a step nearer, but Violet White stood her ground. "I am expecting my students very soon," she said. "I'll not have you here when they arrive. It would alarm and distract them. Please go at once."

The two soldiers burst out laughing. "Alarm her students!" said the one with the lighter hair.

"Yes, indeed, said Violet, her voice like steel. If you have anything further to say to me, say it. But I have nothing to say to you. Now I insist that you leave, immediately!"

The soldiers laughed again, then turned around and headed back for the door.

"Now she's a feisty one!" said the dark-haired soldier.

"Aye. Probably puts damnable ideas into the dirty rebels' heads. I noticed a touch of the king's English in her speech, did you not?"

"Indeed. She's a fine looking wench. I wouldn't mind spending more time in her schoolhouse!" The men laughed loudly as they left, banging the door behind them. Violet leaned against the doorway until their voices faded away, her breath coming harder, her heart beating faster. This was her first face-to-face encounter with the British troops, and she feared it would not be her last. What was happening? She wondered. Where would all this lead?

After the soldiers were out of sight, Violet stood beside her desk, contemplating what had just happened. She had a disturbing feeling – no, knowledge – that they would be back. It was just a question of when.

She sat down on her teacher's stool and idly turned the pages of the book she had brought. Violet remembered her first day, teaching in New Kensington. She knew that her predecessor, a Mr. Dowd, was often cruel to the students, whipping them until they all refused to go to school.

Violet took a different approach, by trying to engage their curiosity; the way Dr. Benjamin Franklin had engaged hers in his laboratory. She had brought books of poetry and prose, mythology and science. Violet knew that her main tasks were to teach the children how to read and write, learn how to add and subtract, and to learn their Bible verses. There was one book in the school, a large Bible that she read from each morning at the beginning of the lessons and after prayers.

Having a woman schoolmistress was quite unusual, since many girls did not go to school at all. Violet's kind approach that appealed to the children's curiosity was also quite radical. Some of the women in the town, like Miss Constance Fisk who ran the dry goods store, grumbled about her fancy ways and said that the state of education in Violet's classroom was sinful. But her students loved her. They were Hannah Hart, Adeline Squires, the Jewell twins, and various farm children who came and went. But none of the slave children attended, nor any of the Indians, nor did Bea Braithwaite, the simple-minded daughter of Mrs. Braithwaite who ran the boarding house in town where Violet lived.

Violet believed all children should go to school, and that they could all learn and enjoy it, too. But she had to accept the way things were in New Kensington, and things were not really so bad. She was comfortable in her room at the boarding house. The schoolhouse was cozy, and she loved her students. She felt she learned as much from them as they did from her. One day the Jewell twins carried a calf to school for her to see. It had been born the day before. Violet marveled at its perfection and stroked it lovingly. The children were not as interested as Violet. They had seen newborn calves many times before.

The parents of her students were kind to her, sometimes sending a jar of beach plum jelly or home baked bread as gifts. But the only one who invited her to her home was the mother of Adeline Squires, whose father was the town judge. They lived in a beautiful brick house on Main Street, with a pianoforte, good paintings, and oriental rugs. It reminded Violet of her father's house on Craven Street in London. Hannah suspected that the other students were too embarrassed to invite her into their humble farmhouses. Violet loved teaching all of them, and was sad when things changed.

She noticed a decline in students' attendance when the presence of the Redcoats had become more obvious. She attributed this to a need for more hands to work in the farms and kitchen gardens to support the burden of housing the quartered soldiers.

When Violet had first arrived, about a year ago, the soldiers had not been a strong presence in New Kensington, preferring larger estates like the William Floyd Estate to the east, with its many buildings, spacious grounds, and plenty of slaves to dote on them. But gradually, first a few, then many Redcoats came into town, followed by more in black coats – the Hessians, who were hired by King George to support his troops. They were generally rude and often drunk. Violet did not understand the German language. She did not like the sound of its guttural rasps, or the leers of the men. As for the Redcoats, she had mixed views. She was British, after all, and spoke in the same accent they did. Some of them seemed so young – her own age, or even younger. She suspected they must miss their homes. What did they have to do with this "revolution," anyway, she wondered. But Violet knew that change was inevitable, and that something bigger than she would ever understand was happening right here, right now, in New Kensington.

She picked up the book she had brought. It was a work by a British woman named Margaret Cavendish. Sometimes she wondered what possible relevance books like this could have for children who worked on farms and at other relentless household tasks. But she answered her doubts with her belief that books of poetry and science and history would open another world to them. The children would learn about faraway places and opportunities. She believed that was what education was all about. She knew these thoughts might be considered blasphemous. The Church said the main point of educating children was to teach them to fear God and to read the Bible. Reverend Windsor had made that clear to her they first day they had met.

The minutes went by and Violet wondered if anyone would show up today. At last the door opened and a slender girl with curls in disarray and a wide smile came into the room.

"Good morning, Hannah," said Violet, smiling back.

"Good morning, Miss White," said Hannah, sitting on the bench closest to the front of the room.

"Did you see anyone else coming? Do you know if Adeline will be here?" asked the teacher as she glanced towards the door, hopeful that Adeline or others would enter.

"No, Miss White," replied Hannah. "Adeline will not be here, and I did not see anyone. I'm quite sure the Jewell twins are working with their mother. She needs them now, with no husband to do the harvesting."

"Well, then, let's get started, just you and me. Let's begin by reading from Proverbs, chapter one. She handed Hannah the Bible. Hannah read,

*The fear of the Lord is the beginning of knowledge, but fools despise wisdom and instruction.*

Hannah's voice was clear and strong. Violet wondered if she sang. She had never heard her sing; yet she was a joyous child. She feared singing was discouraged, but maybe she was wrong. Hannah finished the verse and Violet took the book by Margaret Cavendish from her lap.

"I wanted to show you this book," she said. "Margaret Cavendish was the first woman in England who wrote for publication." She handed the book to Hannah, who opened the small volume. Hannah read,

*Are there other worlds within worlds? Could there be a world in an earring worn by some lady quite unconscious of it?*

"What a fascinating idea," said Hannah. "A world within another world! But is it possible God made many worlds? Does the Bible say anything about that?"

"No, it does not," said Miss White. Once again she realized they were bordering on blasphemy. She changed the subject. "Let's read a poem," she said.

"Have you ever written a poem, Miss White?" asked Hannah.

"Why, yes, I have," said Violet, putting the book down. She remembered the poems she used to write and show to her mother. How she seemed to enjoy them! "But I have not written any lately."

"Could you teach me how to write a poem?"

"Well, I suppose you start by thinking of something that appeals to you, perhaps something beautiful, or perhaps something strong. Then you try to get the essence of it, and put it into words. Just write whatever comes into your mind. You can always change it later."

"But how do I get the rhyme?"

Miss White laughed. "I do not think a poem has to rhyme. After all, some of the most beautiful poetry is in the Bible, and it does not rhyme." Once again she took the Bible from her desk. "Here, in Ecclesiastes:"

Violet read,

*To everything there is a season, and a time to every purpose under the heaven: a time to be born, and a time to die; a time to plant, and a time to pluck up that which is planted; a time to kill, a time to heal; a time to break down, and a time to build up; a time to weep, and a time to laugh; a time to mourn and a time to dance; a time to cast way stones, and a time to gather stones together; a time to embrace, and a time to refrain from embracing; a time to love and a time to hate; a time of war, a time of peace. . .*

Just then there was a tap on the door. Violet looked up. There, standing in the doorway, stood Reverend Windsor. He stepped into the room, his large frame blocking out the light of the doorway. Then he spoke. "There were soldiers at Hart's Tavern who were bragging about coming into the schoolhouse," he said, his voice resonant and rich. "I happened to be passing by and I just thought I'd check on things. Is everything all right?"

"Why, yes, thank you," said Violet.

Reverend Windsor stepped fully into the room, put his hands on his hips, and with a kind of swagger walked over to them.

"Well, I am pleased to see that you seem to be deeply engaged in reading the Bible, of which I heartily approve."

"Thank you, Reverend Windsor," said Violet. She smiled disarmingly, holding the Reverend's gaze as she quickly turned pages to a different section of the Bible, thinking that perhaps Ecclesiastes was not the best choice at the moment.

"I will be on my way," said the Reverend. "Good day, ladies. I will see you in church."

Reverend Windsor tipped his hat and left. Violet and Hannah looked at each other and smiled a little guiltily, as if sharing some secret.

# Chapter Eight

Goody Garlicke swept the porch of her tidy, but small cottage. She hummed a little tune, one that her husband had taught her many years ago. The song was about the sun, the sea, and the sky, all of which had been so important to him. Right now, in the late afternoon of a brilliant September day, the sun was low, the air was crisp and dry, and the sea sparkled in the distance.

When she was finished with her sweeping Goody went inside the house, but propped open the door with a log to allow fresh air to enter. Soon she would have to keep the door closed, because in a month or two the first snow would fall.

Inside the house a huge fireplace took up nearly the entire far wall, and another, smaller fireplace was in the room beyond that. Colorful rag rugs covered the bare boards of the floor. Goody grasped one of these and dragged it out the door, where she tossed it over the clothesline and gave it several good whacks with the rug beater. She would drag the rugs out again in spring to get out the winter soot and dust.

I'm not as young as I used to be, thought the old woman as she put down the rug beater and headed for the porch. She decided to boil some water for a nice cup of chamomile tea. Goody grew the herb herself. She didn't know anyone who had enjoyed a real cup of tea since a band of colonists in Boston dumped British tea into the harbor a few years back to protest taxes.

Goody ambled over to the small back room to fetch the chamomile leaves that were on shelves containing jars of ground roots, herbs and spices. There were also jars and pots containing remedies made from ingredients that were Goody's secret. She readily admitted she was not a doctor. Doctor Myers was the town physician. He treated broken bones, the croup, and bled people who needed it. But when Dr. Myers' treatments did not work, or when someone wanted to be sure they were doing everything possible for whatever was ailing them, he or she would make the trip to the edge of Melancholy Hollow and pay a visit to Goody Garlicke. Goody knew many of the native people who lived here. They were a peaceful lot, surviving by fishing, clamming, and farming. From time to time they came to see her, too. She believed that a soft poultice of mashed beans applied to an arthritic joint would bring relief. An ointment made of earthworms soothed strained muscles. Boiled potatoes cleansed hands and prevented the spread of disease. In fact, boiling in general seemed to keep people healthy. That is why she boiled all of her drinking water, and told young mothers to boil their water, to keep their children healthy. She also had a way with animals, and made house calls to help birth a lamb or a colt. She owned several cats and two dogs, which stayed in the house with her in wintertime.

Soon the water was simmering in the kettle above the hearth, and Goody poured it over the leaves. She took her cup and headed for the rocker on her porch, settling down with a pillow behind her back. Soon the melody she was humming earlier began to drift through her mind again. She seldom thought of her young husband these days, but when the air turned brisk and the sky was such a brilliant blue that it almost hurt one's eyes, well . . . the thoughts of him intruded and the song came to her lips.

She was almost finished with her tea when she noticed a spot of red coming down the road -- no, two spots. She got up from her chair and leaned on her broom, watching as two British soldiers came into view. She was used to their presence. They had been around Melancholy Hollow since the skirmish with the Indians and the French, although no battles were fought in these parts. Goody observed the two men, who came closer. How uncomfortable they looked, she thought, in their lobster-red coats. They were young and handsome, far from their homes, just boys, really. The old woman shook her head. Why must young people suffer wars? She wondered. Would there never be an end to them?

Goody's eyesight was poor and she did not read much, but she knew what was going on. She made a trip into town about once a week and looked at the broadsheets that were posted on the trees in the town square. She talked to the people in the markets, and one day had observed the young new school marm walking from Mrs. Braithwaite's boarding house to the schoolhouse. A beauty, that one, thought Goody. She sensed a kind of restlessness in the town. She could almost smell it in the air. Goody had lived through a lot. She knew that anything could happen at any time, like the day the moon passed in front of the sun and the sky grew dark, and people said it was a sign from God. But most days were the same.

The soldiers were now in front of the cabin. Goody stood in her doorway, regarding them. The wind whipped around her dusty black skirts.

"Hallo, Old Mistress," said the dark haired one. "Have you a glass of ale for two thirsty soldiers?"

Goody shook her head. "Nay, I do not drink ale. I can offer you some water. There is a pump by the side of the house."

They got down from their horses and led them to the trough by the pump.

Goody eyed them warily. While their horses drank, they came back to her doorway. "What manner of cottage is this?" He turned to his companion, the soldier with light brown hair, and tilted his chin toward the doorway. "Let us in to inspect. Make way, old woman."

Goody did not move from the doorway. "'Tis just the humble home of an old woman and her cats," she said, and broke into a violent fit of coughing, allowing spittle to drip a little down her chin, which she then wiped away with the back of her hand. "I'd better go inside now and take herbs for this cough." Goody broke into another fit of hacking and wheezing.

The soldiers backed away. They feared contagion, and disease was a constant threat. They hesitated, and Goody started coughing, even more violently than before. The soldiers then moved toward their horses. Goody entered her cottage and closed the door. She looked through her window and smiled her gap-toothed smile when she saw the soldiers quickly mount their horses and ride toward town. The fear of typhus, typhoid and the dreaded smallpox were enough to keep anyone away. Goody kept a clean house, and was quite healthy, but the soldiers did not know that. They had not drunk from her well, nor entered her home. The soldiers were probably on their way to the alehouse, right now.

# Chapter Nine

Wyanjoy waded out into the Great South Bay, pushing her canoe. The clear water was shallow for a good distance, with small waves that lapped at her toes and legs, eventually reaching her waist. Then she leaned against the side of the little boat and eased herself into it. Picking up a paddle from the inside of the boat she made her way south, towards the barrier island that separated the Great Bay from the ocean, protecting the mainland from its huge waves.

The earlier fog had lifted somewhat, but Wyanjoy could not yet make out the shape of the land. Nevertheless, she was not worried. She followed the shrieking gulls that dove beneath the surface and came up with fishes in their beaks. The bay was calm; the color of smoke, but Wyanjoy knew that could change like the wind. The bay could be calm and yielding one moment, and fierce and belligerent the next. She had experienced all its moods and knew how much of a risk she was willing to take.

She paddled out, alternating two strokes on each side of the canoe, until eventually the barrier beach came into view. Along its edge grew masses of reeds, scrub pine, shadblow and holly. Later, if she had time, Wyanjoy would gather some sassafras roots and beach plums that grew abundantly between the bay and the ocean. But now she had something more important to do. She slid the canoe onto the beach, well away from the water's edge. Then she removed a basket and a forked stick from the canoe. She tied the basket around her waist with a narrow length of deer hide and allowed it to float on the calm water, and waded into the water until it was almost up to her chest. She knew the exact spot she wanted. Using the stick as a probe, she stirred up the bay bottom and used her feet to dig down. Clams were plentiful here. Their upturned ridges were easy to locate buried in the soft sand. Less common were the rougher oyster shells. Wyanjoy wanted both. Not only did they provide food for her family, occasionally, she found a small, perfectly round stone in one of the oysters. The stone glowed like the moon, and Wyanjoy knew it had magic properties. The white men were crazy for these stones and she could trade them in their market for many things.

For two hours Wyanjoy trod along the bay bottom, putting her foot over a clam or oyster, then reaching down to pick it up and put it in her basket. Her back grew tired, but she continued until the basket was full. She saw that little waves were coming up on the bay, a sign that the weather would shift. She'd better return. She would wait to gather her plants until next time, but not too long. The next moon would bring colder weather, and her belly would be large with the child she carried. This would probably be her last trip to the collect clams and oysters before the first snow came. They would keep in baskets of briny water, to last through the winter. Her sisters would bring home eels, her brother, perhaps, a deer. The other women of the village would be making corn meal from the first harvest, and corn soup. The girls would have gathered the last of the blueberries and blackberries. There was plenty to eat, for now.

Wyanjoy glided to the shore and dragged the boat onto the beach, a short distance to the marshy area beyond the sand. When the land turned marshy again she slid the canoe through the reeds, steadying her basket on the floor of the canoe. She moved silently, but the birds sensed her presence. Three red winged blackbirds took flight, screeching angrily, their ebony bodies and bright red wings darting through the air. Wyanjoy trudged on. She was getting cold now, in the late afternoon. Dusk was approaching. Her deerskin skirt was soaked through. At last she reached the clearing at the end of the reeds and the small cove where the boat was again free to float. Wyanjoy got in and paddled a short distance to the other side, where an overhang of trees and vines provided a shelter for her canoe. She pushed it under a willow tree, tethered the canoe, removed her basket, and prepared to make the rest of her journey on foot, back to her family, east to their village. She walked quickly to the main road. It was getting dark now, but Wyanjoy was sure of the way. She balanced the basket of clams and oysters on her hip as she walked along, gracefully and swiftly despite the load she was carrying.

She no longer heard the cry of the red winged blackbirds, but suddenly a different flash of red and black came into view. Two tall white men in startling red coats, with weapons hanging from their shoulders appeared on the road, weaving slightly as they walked. They must be soldiers of the white men's king, she realized, who had pushed their way into the homes of the white people of New Kensington. She did not understand much of the language of these people, which sounded like the yips and barks of the foxes. But she sensed that the white people of the village did not like these red-coated men. The merchants she traded with and the white farmers did not smile at these soldiers. They seemed to raise their hackles like bobcats at the red-coated men.

Suddenly they were face to face with her, drunkenly laughing. Wyanjoy tried to ignore them, hurrying faster down the road, but their legs were too long, and soon they caught up with her.

"What 'ave we here?" bellowed the black-haired one.

"Looks like a savage to me," said the other. Wyanjoy felt fear for the first time. She did not like their leering looks, the shiny blades of their swords. What would they do to her?

The two swaggered over to her, right up close. Wyanjoy could smell the stench of their breath and gripped her basket closer. She started to run, but they followed, soon catching up with her. "What've ye got in the basket, young savage?" Wyanjoy did not understand his words, but she feared the tone of his voice. She grasped her basket more tightly and tried to get away. But the black haired-one held her arms and pushed her to the ground. The clams and oysters scattered everywhere, and the two men laughed loudly as Wyanjoy scrambled to gather them up.

"Go away!" she yelled in her language. "Leave me alone!" But the men waited until she had gathered all the shellfish, taunting her all the while. She was glad she did not understand their words.

"Well, I guess it's time we headed back," said the light-haired one."

"Ah, yes," said the other. "And wouldn't these fish make a tasty treat with our pints of ale?" He pulled the basket out of Wyanjoy's arms and thrust her away. She almost fell again, but managed to stand her ground, anger growing inside her like the whirlwinds that blew in the dunes of the barrier beach. She stood there, her eyes narrowed, her fists clasped at her sides as the two soldiers staggered away, back down the street from where they had come.

Wyanjoy felt a stirring in her belly. She worried about this child. Would it be safe in a land where men stole the food of women and children? She turned and walked empty handed, back to her village.

# Chapter Ten

As twilight approached, Secatogue marsh was as black as the eels that inhabited the mud of its depths. Wyanjoy walked home, alongside the marsh, empty handed. She was shaken by her encounter with the Redcoats, and was tired and cold. As she looked out over the marsh, she saw lights flicker. They appeared to dance across the surface of the reeds, and disappear, only to reappear a few feet away. Wyanjoy took comfort in these pale lights of the marsh, the will o' the wisp, believing they were small spirits who wished to guide her way.

She quickened her steps for the last half-mile until she reached the entryway to the thatched house that she shared with her mother and sisters. Her chest was heaving and she felt chilled to the bone. A large fire crackled in the center of the single room. She was glad to see the women with their long braids and soft eyes who silently brought her warm broth. They looked at her empty hands and said nothing.

"I want to see Winnequaheagh," said Wyanjoy. Winnequaheagh was the sachem of the tribe.

"He is not here, Wyanjoy," said a gray-haired woman, who was her mother. "What is wrong, my daughter?"

"Two white men in red coats took all my quahaug and oysters. They were drunk and crude. I want to tell Sachem that he must not help them in their quarrels with the white farmers. They are not our friends."

The white haired woman nodded. "I will tell him," she said quietly. "Now I must go to Shoqua. Her baby is very sick. I do not expect him to live."

Wyanjoy nodded and sat before the fire. Perhaps the lights of the spirits she saw over the black swamp were a sign that the baby would soon join them. Death was common in the tribe. Diseases that were unknown to the ancestors were becoming more and more common. Plagues were brought here with the white men along with their red coats and their weapons.

The Seacatogues and the white farmers got along well before the men in red came to stay. They did not make war the way some of the other Algonquian tribes did. The Seacatogues were farmers too, planting crops like the white farmers, sometimes side by side. Wyanjoy had grown to enjoy trading in their market. She was particularly adept at weaving tight baskets from the marsh grass. Along with these she traded clams, oysters, fish, lobsters, belts of wampum, and, above all, the pearls she occasionally found inside an oyster. These were her most valuable possessions, and they brought a good price. In return for one or two pearls she got cloth, tools and medicine for the children.

Now Wyanjoy's mother and sisters left her alone. As she sat in front of the warm, drowsy fire, Wyanjoy closed her eyes and let her mind run free. An idea started to form. She realized that if she and her unborn child were to survive, she would need to prepare, and do something extraordinary. But first she would try to help Shoqua's baby.

She got up from her spot near the fire, and changed into dry clothes. Next she went to the far corner of the room and lifted the edge of the woven mat that covered the floor. The floor was solidly packed earth, except in this corner, where Wyanjoy dug down an inch or so. She felt the little leather drawstring pouch she had hidden there and pulled it out. From inside the pouch she took a small, folded piece of cloth and spread it on the floor. She opened it carefully, revealing a dozen lustrous pearls of various sizes, all of them white except for two gray ones and one large, black pearl. She selected two of the white pearls and tied them into another small square of cloth, which she slipped into a pocket inside her waistband. She returned the remaining pearls to their hiding place. Then once again Wyanjoy ventured outside.

A full moon, golden as a melon, rose over Secatogue marsh and the Great Bay. It was the fall harvest moon, when everything is brought into the storehouses: the sheaves of precious corn, beans, baskets of potatoes and squash. Its reflection glinted upon the slate black water, sending out slivers of light that looked like darting silver fishes. A lone gull cried in the distance, then was silent. The air was chill. In a few weeks the winds would howl, the sleet and snow would slash down, and waves would rip into the shores of Great Bay and the barrier beach until by mid-winter the water would freeze into a solid sheet of ice.

Wyanjoy hurried past the marsh and through the meadow that rose up beyond the reeds. At the top of the hill was the cottage of a white woman she had seen in the market. She had heard that this woman had special herbs and medicines that could cure diseases. The moonlight lit Wyanjoy's path, but she was also thankful for the dark shadows in which she could hide. She was afraid to be seen by the British soldiers. That is how it is in life, she thought. Light and darkness each have their place.

After a while Wyanjoy saw the cottage in the moonlight. She made her way up the hill through weeds and grass and approached the hut cautiously. Would the old woman answer her request? Could she make herself understood?

The cottage was set among several trees, the only ones in the meadow. It was made of logs with brush stuffed between them, not the typical house of the white farmers. Smoke rose from a chimney in the middle of the roof. On both sides of the house were rows of vegetables, ready to be harvested. Meadow flowers, gone to seed, and milkweed grew wild around the rest of the house. Wyanjoy knocked on the door, lightly at first, then harder when no one answered. After several minutes the door opened and a gray-haired woman in dark clothing stood there with a shotgun at her side.

"What is it?" she asked, her eyes narrowing. Wyanjoy sensed that the woman's eyesight was poor. "What do you want?"

"I am Wyanjoy. I know you from the marketplace. I hear that you are wise and have medicine."

Goody stared at the young Indian woman for nearly a full minute. She noted the thick, smooth hair done in two long braids, and the skin the color of walnuts. She noticed the expressive, large dark eyes. By the look of her, Goody believed Wyanjoy could be a member of her husband's tribe.

Then she noticed the swelling of her belly beneath the layers of deerskin she wore.

"Are you alone?" asked Goody.

"Yes."

"Then come in."

Goody led Wyanjoy to a rough-hewn table near the fire. Shelves lined the walls on all sides of the room. On either side of the fireplace were what appeared to be a sleeping nook and a pantry. Wyanjoy took all this in, and suddenly relaxed in her chair. She had walked a long way this evening, and it felt good to sit down.

As if sensing Wyanjoy's fatigue Goody walked over to the small stove, poured out a large mug of herbal tea, and handed it to Wyanjoy, who took the cup gratefully, inhaling its fragrance before sipping it. "Thank you," she said. "It is good."

"I grow the leaves myself," said Goody, watching Wyanjoy drink the tea, wondering if she were hungry. "We no longer drink British tea. But I suppose you would not know about that." Wyanjoy sipped the warm tea Goody Garlicke had given her. She recognized its mild, flowery flavor, made from an herb that grew prevalently near the marsh. Wyanjoy felt comfortable, but her eyes darted around the room. She had never been in a white person's home before. It was warmer and sturdier than the thatched houses of her people. Goody sat quietly while Wyanjoy sipped the tea. She then put some dry biscuits on the table, which Wyanjoy ate quickly. Her hunger grew greater every day, as her child grew inside her, and often there was not enough to eat at her home.

As if reading her thoughts Goody pointed to Wyanjoy's belly and raised her hand slightly, palm up, to indicate a question. "I see you are with child. When do you expect it to come?"

Wyanjoy did not answer, but traced two circles on the table top with her fingertip. Two full moons.

Goody nodded. Winter. It would be difficult for this young woman, she thought. She knew about the native people who lived along the marsh. She had seen their grass houses. She knew they were poor and had to eke out a living. Their prominence in this area was coming to an end because their numbers were dying out, just as her husband had died. Goody expected that the white settlers were somehow responsible for the diseases that were rampant throughout the Indian settlement.

Goody got up and put another log on the fire, causing a few sparks to fly out. One landed on her old cat, Wacket, causing him to leap up and hiss. Then he shook himself and settled down in the very same spot. Wyanjoy smiled, something she rarely did, revealing two rows of strong, white teeth, like rows of pearls. Not one of them was missing. Goody was suddenly impressed with her beauty. She never did discover the secret to good, strong teeth. They were rare among the colonists. Goody had quite a few teeth missing herself, one of them in front.

Goody decided she liked this young Indian, although she did not completely trust her. People said they could pull out a knife at any time and steal everything you had. Yet, what did Goody have to steal? Nothing. Her greatest treasure was in her mind – her knowledge of the medicines and potions and luck charms and rituals that could cure and curse. She felt confident that this young woman meant her no harm. "Why have you come to me?" she asked finally.

At last Wyanjoy said, "My sister's baby is ill. None of our medicines work. I heard you have special medicine." Wyanjoy could not explain that two more members of her tribe had died this week, one of them the father of her unborn child. She feared she could be next. The strange sickness with its sweating and weakness came quickly and took its victims the way a predator takes its prey. And what of her unborn child? Would it survive?

Goody shook her head. I have few remedies to help babies. Many die. There is little I can do."

"Please," Wyanjoy's eyes seemed even larger now, pleading, "Please try. He is my sister's only child." She reached into her pocket and took out the pearls. "These are a token of my trust in you," she said in her own language, pushing the cloth across the table.

Goody eyed the pearls. They would fetch a good price. "I must see the baby before I can help, if I can help at all. Do you understand?"

Goody was not a doctor, but she knew the town doctor would not see the Indian. Also, Goody was not conventional. She did not believe in bloodletting, especially for infants, nor many of the remedies Dr. Myers prescribed. He was fine for setting broken bones and pulling teeth, but she did not trust his powders and pills. She had her own, and she believed they worked just as well.

Goody got up from her chair and went over to her shelves. She thought, what could be wrong with the baby? She suspected it was the weakening disease common to infants among the Indians. She selected a jar from her shelf. This would help control diarrhea, she knew, but the baby would need other nutrients and medicines. She took down a jar and poured out a small pile of leaves into a small scrap of cloth, which she tied with a string. It contained leaves of yarrow, violet blossoms and wild peppermint. She wrapped the medicine in a square of cloth and gave it to Wyanjoy. "Here is some medicine made from herbs and roots that can help your sister's child. Boil this in water and give it to the child in small sips. Bring him to me tomorrow and I will see what else I can do."

Wyanjoy drank down the rest of the tea and reluctantly got up. She did not want to leave the warmth and light of this fine room. She wrapped her deerskin around her shoulders and faced Goody. Inclining her head in respect she said, "Kway don owa," meaning thank you, and departed.

The next day Wyanjoy did not come. The air had grown cold, and rain poured down, creating rivulets of water from the hill where Goody's house stood down to the marsh. Goody told herself that perhaps the young Indian would wait for clear weather before bringing the baby. Days went by and Goody watched for the young Indian. By the seventh day Goody realized that the baby had died and that Wyanjoy would not come.

# Chapter Eleven

Hannah liked to ride Honeycomb, the gentler of the two horses her father owned. She rode on the path that ran alongside the black marshes that were part of the landscape of the Great Bay. The brisk, cool breeze felt good, for the sun was strong. The fog that had risen earlier in the morning had completely gone. As Honeycomb trotted along the path, Hannah glimpsed the bay where there were small openings between the reeds. Where the land dropped down to Melancholy Hollow, the lowest part of the shore, the bay became entirely visible. Parts of "the hollow," as people called the spot, were even below sea level when the tide rose high during a full moon. A few rocky outcroppings existed near the shore, making it treacherous for those unfamiliar with the bay.

Today the water was still and silver, like a mirror. During storms it could churn and thrash into a greenish maelstrom, tossing up salt froth, with waves heaving back and forth onto the shore. Hannah respected this water and never ventured into it alone, the way some people did. Girls were not encouraged to swim, anyway, so at best she would wade up to her knees in hot weather.

Today she observed one of the local Indians pushing her log boat into the water. She had seen the young woman before, in the Main Street of New Kensington, trading wampum necklaces and finely woven baskets for cloth, dye and other things. Hannah watched with admiration as the young woman tossed her basket into the small boat and then jumped in, paddling with strong arms out into the bay. For some reason Hannah found herself saying a little prayer, "God protect this woman, who goes out alone on the Great Bay. Keep the water calm for her."

Hannah nudged Honeycomb and continued along the path. When it narrowed she turned inland, to the meadow that gently rose over a hill that led to the woods. Dry grass now stuck out in tufts along the hillside, along with white-topped wild carrots and the tall, golden flowers that bloomed in autumn. Hannah loved this meadow, especially in the spring, when wildflowers of all colors bloomed, turning it into a brilliant, rainbow-colored bouquet.

In the distance Hannah saw old Goody Garlicke, kneeling down beside one of her cows. Many people believed Goody was a witch. Hannah and Adeline discussed her sometimes, out of earshot of others, because it was considered impolite and foolish to talk about witches. Hannah knew about the witch trouble in Salem, Massachusetts that had happened less than a hundred years ago, when twenty innocent persons were hanged for witchcraft. Miss White had told the pupils it was tragic and nonsense, but Hannah knew that many people still believed in witches. Evie, Hannah's slave, especially, feared Goody Garlicke and always crossed herself if she saw her in town.

Goody appeared to be examining the cow's left front leg, lifting it gently, rubbing it with a cloth, and then scraping it with a knife. Such behavior was indeed strange. A little shiver ran down Hannah's spine. Hannah turned toward the bay again, breathing in the mild, slightly salty air. A gull cried overhead. The sun seemed suddenly low in the sky. Hannah felt the urge to leave. She dug her knees sharply into Honeycomb's flanks, sending her into a gallop. She turned the horse back toward the bay, knowing that the sun, air and sky could change at any moment. But for now, she would just enjoy the ride.

Goody Garlicke, meanwhile, also observed Hannah that mild September day. She was out in the meadow, checking on her herbs and flowers, enjoying the warm sun. There would not be many more days like this one, she knew. In the distance she saw Hannah, riding a small honey-colored mare. Squinting against the sun, she thought, Ah, that's Hannah Hart, the innkeeper's daughter. She's a pretty thing. She shouldn't be out riding alone with the soldiers all about.

Goody turned around and saw Matilda, her milk cow, at the north end of the meadow. The cow seemed to be favoring her left front leg -- limping a bit. She walked across the meadow to where the cow stood. Patting Matilda on the head and speaking softly to her, Goody lifted the cow's leg to take a look. She pulled a handkerchief out of her apron and cleaned off some dried blood from a wound. There was a nasty, oozing lesion upon her leg and two others on her udders. It was cowpox! Goody studied the wounds. They appeared similar to the pockmarks of the victims she had seen with the smallpox disease. Goody had heard about inoculation. It was said that General Washington was even inoculating his troops. Goody had an idea.

Goody often tried new herbs and ointments, applying the potions to herself, or to one of her animals. Sometimes there was no reaction; other times the result was marked and sometimes surprising, like the time she applied a salve made from henbane to the base of Wacket's tail in an attempt to rid her of fleas. The poor cat licked her tail, then spun around like a top until Goody caught her and washed off the potion. More successful than the henbane flea-cure were her potions for headache, stomachache, and sleeplessness. A calming brew of chamomile and peppermint usually cured these ills.

More serious, however, was the scourge of smallpox that was sweeping through the colonies. Goody herself had seen its victims – Indians and colonists alike who were covered with ugly pockmarks, exuding the distinctive, sickly sweet smell of the disease.

She led Matilda to the barn and went to the house, returning to Matilda's stall with a dull knife and a walnut. She cracked open the walnut, ate its contents, and then saved the two matched shells. Now, speaking softly to Matilda, she scraped away at the pockmark on the cow's leg, removing a small amount of debris from the wound. This she scraped into the walnut shell, a good container for so small an amount of a potion. Giving Matilda another affectionate pat, Goody got up stiffly from her crouching position and made her way back to the house.

Once inside, Goody got her sewing kit. Then she lifted the sleeve of her blouse and washed her left arm above the elbow with lye soap and water. Next, she lit a candle and held her longest sewing needle over the flame. Goody was not sure why she did this, but she suspected that the fire somehow purified the needle. She took the needle and scraped four small cuts into her arm, first vertically, then four more crisscrossing those. Blood billowed from the scratches, leaving a wound about the size of a coin. Goody carefully opened the walnut and poked the needle into the cowpox matter she had deposited there. Then she scratched the needle into the wound.

She touched the needle into the walnut shell and then onto her arm, again and again, until she was sure that much of the cowpox ended up in her arm. When she was finished she tied a clean handkerchief loosely over the wound. Then she covered the nutshell and placed it carefully on her shelf. If the inoculation worked, Goody decided, the wound should scab over in a few days. Then she would be protected from smallpox. If that Indian girl, Wyanjoy, came back with the sick baby, she would inoculate them, too. Goody felt a kinship with the young Indian.

With a smile of satisfaction, Goody returned to her chair by the fire. Wacket leaped into her lap, purring and kneading her paws. Goody smiled at the memory of the poor cat doing its wild dance in circles. "I must try another remedy for fleas," she thought.

# Chapter Twelve

Violet White looked around her plain, clean room. A low bed covered with a colorful patchwork quilt faced the small fireplace, where an oval rug woven from fabric scraps covered the wood floor. A small chest and mirror were against one wall, as well as a narrow wardrobe for hanging clothes. On the opposite side of the room, under the window, was a desk. A large trunk was beside it. The room was crowded – nothing like her room back in London. But it was what Violet called home, here with Mrs. Braithwaite, her landlady, and Mrs. Braithwaite's daughter, Bea.

Mealtimes were generally quiet, because Mrs. Braithwaite, who always dressed in black, was still in mourning for her husband who had died two years ago. And despite Violet's efforts to engage her in conversation, Bea rarely spoke at all. People said she was not quite right in the head – "simple minded," Miss Constance Fisk had told Violet one day, when Violet had gone shopping in the dry goods store Miss Fisk owned. Violet was determined to try to get to know the girl better.

But today, a wave of homesickness washed over her as she sat down on her bed. Is this the kind of life I want? She wondered. Is this the life of adventure I dreamed of when I left Father and the comforts of Craven Street in London?

Violet's father was a well-respected doctor in the heart of London. Again she read his most recent letter, a few short newsy paragraphs about his activities with Catherine, Violet's stepmother. They were well. Dr. Benjamin Franklin had left London, and her father missed their after-dinner conversations. He asked how she was doing with her students, and when she would be returning to Craven Street. They missed her.

Violet stared out the small window that looked out upon the Main Street of New Kensington. The colonial town was a far cry from London; the boarding house was humble compared to the well-appointed home on Craven Street. She remembered the wide, polished oak staircase in the entry foyer, where the maids bobbed a curtsey as she made her way to breakfast in the dining room, with its fine English bone china and Bohemian crystal. She remembered the maids and her parents applauding when she was a tiny girl, as she plucked the fattest raisin from the top of a scone. It was a game they often played. Violet smiled at the memory.

Violet remembered their neighbor, Dr. Franklin, the statesman and scientist, who occasionally came to visit her father. While her father sipped a glass of sherry Dr. Franklin would lift his glass of ale and the two would engage in lively conversation. Violet smiled again as she remembered how Dr. Franklin had declared, "Beer is proof that God loves us and wants us to be happy!"

One day he had explained to Violet that lightning was electrical. He showed her and Dr. White one of the metal-tipped kites he had used to "capture the fire of heaven," as he put it, sending the kites aloft over the River Thames during thunderstorms, proving that electricity had a negative charge. Their good neighbor and friend had even invented the stove that stood in the center of her classroom!

She remembered the day Dr. Franklin had invited Violet and her father to see his laboratory, which was located at the back of his fine house. Inside there were all sorts of strange tubes, vials, burners and implements, and papers piled everywhere.

"What is that?" asked Violet, pointing to a series of rods of different lengths and diameters.

"Lightning rods," my dear, said Ben Franklin. "When I have perfected them they will be placed on all the great structures of London – the houses of Parliament, St. Paul's Cathedral . . . These rods will capture the electricity and send it safely to the ground so the precious, historical buildings will be safe from the forces of Nature."

Dr. Franklin had indeed perfected the lightning rods and had them affixed to the buildings he mentioned, much to the displeasure of King George, who did not comprehend Dr. Franklin's theories. At that time there was already talk of trouble in the colonies, and shortly after Violet's visit to his laboratory Benjamin Franklin left London for good and returned to Philadelphia.

Violet had to admit that Benjamin Franklin was one of the main motivations for her coming to the New World. He told Violet and her father about the spaciousness and beauty of the colonies, the sense of freedom that prevailed among its people. But the actual day Violet made her decision to leave London was etched in her mind. It was the day her young stepmother, Catherine, knocked on Violet's bedroom door and said they needed to talk.

Catherine was a beautiful young woman, only ten years older than Violet, with dark, almost black hair and startling green eyes. Violet remembered on that day the pupils of those eyes were like sharp pinpricks. Catherine perched on the white ruffled chair opposite the four-poster bed, upon which Violet sat in silence until finally Catherine cleared her throat and said, "I should get right to the point. Your father and I are concerned about your future. We think it is time you started to look for a husband."

Violet drew in her breath, momentarily speechless. Then she laughed. "Look for a husband? Whatever for? I am not ready for a husband!"

Catherine did not smile. "Your father cannot support you forever," she said. "Don't you want a home of your own?"

Violet realized that Catherine was not joking, and regarded her warily. What was her game? Catherine was always effusive and smiling in Dr. White's presence when she spoke to Violet, but now her voice was as dry as autumn leaves. Violet replied slowly, "I suppose I do want a home of my own one day. But right now I am still studying. I want to do more than keep a house.

Dr. Franklin is teaching me about science. I want to learn about history, I want to travel . . ."

"Then perhaps you should seek employment," said Catherine abruptly.

Violet said nothing. She looked into the eyes of her stepmother, who had married Joseph White just last year, after he had been widowed for so long. Violet could swear Catherine had bewitched him. Her father had met her at a dinner party and they were married six months later. What was she holding back?

As if reading her mind, Catherine said, "I am expecting a child." Violet was stunned. A child! A stepbrother or sister! Violet had no siblings. A smile broke out over her face.

"That is wonderful, Catherine!" she exclaimed, rising to hug her. But Catherine's embrace was cold.

"You need to decide about your future soon," she said, pulling away from Violet. "Your father will have other things to think about when the baby comes." Then she left the room.

Yes, that meeting was the catalyst that brought Violet White to the New World. She supposed she ought to feel grateful to Catherine. She was able to locate a ship departing from London within a matter of weeks, and secure her teaching position and her room at the boarding house through the Church's connection to Reverend Windsor. But Violet missed home. There was no getting around that, especially since soldiers of her own King and country had set foot in her schoolhouse and had threatened her.

"This is a strange turn of events, indeed," she said to herself, as she folded her father's letter and put it in her letterbox. "I wonder what will happen next."

# Chapter Thirteen

Today was ale making day, and Hannah was up early. Evie had set the water to boil in the huge cauldron over the fire outside. It would take six people all day to pick the hops, which would amount to only about five pounds of the dried cones. This would yield enough ale for about six months. There were still four casks in the cellar from the last batch they made six months ago. Ale was made twice a year, in the spring and fall, to ensure a good supply for the year.

Hart's Tavern had a long tradition of ale making. Hannah's great grandfather, Ezekiel Redmund Hart, who had built the inn in the late 1600s, was acquainted with a brewer in Massachusetts who taught him the process of making ale. Over time, the Hart family recipes for beer and ale evolved, and were kept secret.

In cities in the 1600s, beer was a necessity because most water was polluted. Now, in 1775, drinking water came from wells that provided cold, clear, and pure water, so ale was no longer a nutritional necessity. People drank it for enjoyment, and the ale served at Hart's Tavern was known as the best for miles around – even better, some said, than the brew served at the famous Fraunces Tavern in New York City.

While the slaves picked the cones that that grew on vines climbing up trellises in the hops garden, Hannah prepared the herbs needed for flavoring. She picked from her herb garden bunches of burnet, betony, thyme, marjoram, elder flowers, rosemary, sage, chamomile and mint. She arranged the herbs on two boards that rested on saw horses not far from the cauldron. Certain herbs would be used for different brews, like the dark, herbal ale known as *mumm*. Some of the herbs would be added to the casks after the fermentation process. There were bitter herbs, such as horehound, sage, nettle, gentian and milk thistle, and aromatic herbs like rosemary, hyssop and lavender. Flowering herbs could also be added, such as juniper, spruce and borage.

While some of the slaves picked the hop cones, others worked on threshing and winnowing. Threshing meant separating the grains from the dried seed heads. To do this the cones were placed in a long cloth that the slaves hit over and over again with brooms. Winnowing required separating the grains from bits of straw. This was hard work. The slaves began before sunrise and worked all day until the process was finished, with only a short break for the midday meal. Peter Hart would trade ale in payment to Mr. Bedkin, the vintner, for the slaves he had borrowed today.

Mr. Bedkin owned the vineyard just to the north of New Kensington. At grape harvesting time, all available people in the area gathered at the vineyard to pick grapes from the rows and rows of vines. It was a large harvest, requiring many hands. Even the children helped.

At Hart's Tavern, there was just one row of grape vines at the far end of the garden, along with a few patches of rhubarb and strawberries, which Hannah harvested to make jam. There was not enough of this fruit to make wine, so Peter Hart also traded his ale for Mr. Bedkin's wine.

Three of Mr. Bedkin's slaves were named Daisy, Liddie, and Camartha. Their faces shone like black pearls under their white mobcaps as they hauled bucket after bucket of water to add to the slow boiling brew. Evie stirred it with a long stick while the others added cups of molasses and bunches of barley.

Soon the air was filled with the pleasant aroma of ale. This smell was comforting to Hannah, who had grown up with the earthy aroma of fresh hops, and the yeasty smell of the brew. It was a part of her life at the Inn. She was accustomed to the bitter taste of ale, although she much preferred to drink milk, or sweet water, a kind of drink made with honey.

Today the weather was unseasonably warm, and Hannah had felt like a wilting lily when she stood near the heat of the fire after picking hops all morning. Now she rested under a tree with a book in her lap, not far from the slave women who were talking to one another. Some of their words were in a language Hannah could not understand, African words that mingled with their own dialect of English. Apparently they were unaware of Hannah's presence, or maybe they did not care that she was there. Hannah held up her book, pretending to read, but instead listened to what they said.

"They still didn't catch Blanchard. He's no doubt joined the Redcoats," said Camartha, who was the oldest of the three.

"The Redcoats?"

"Yes. Gone to New York City, I'm thinking. Once you join up with the Redcoats you are free. No more master, just fight this war."

"Women too?" asked Evie. Rarely had Hannah seen Evie this animated. Her eyes were wide. She could barely stand still.

"No, no women Redcoats. But women can get free. I heard about a woman in New York City who became half-free at seventeen. She opened a bakery there, mostly making wedding cakes for white people, but she still had to pay tax to her former owner. She helped all the orphaned children, both black and white, who lived nearby. Some say she's raised round about forty-five young'uns by now."

The women worked quietly as they seemed to mull over the idea of a half-freed slave woman who raised so many children by baking cakes.

"Maybe she could help me," said Evie quietly, breaking the silence.

Hannah's ears strained to catch every word as she buried her face in her book. What did Evie mean, help her?" Then Evie glanced over her shoulder. Her suspicions must have been aroused because she and the other three women moved away from the kettle and picked up their water buckets, walking out of Hannah's earshot. They were up to something; Hannah felt sure about that.

They moved slowly to the large oak tree near the barn. Daisy glanced back over her shoulder as they walked, until they sat themselves under the shady tree. Hannah watched as Camartha made broad gestures with her arms and hands while the other women nodded, apparently in agreement. Sometimes she pointed to the west.

A moment later Mr. Bedkin and Hannah's father appeared in the wagon, which was filled with another load of hops, molasses, and empty ale barrels. It was time to pour the finished ale into the kegs and start another batch. The wagon stopped near the fireplace and the two men got out. Hannah's father proceeded to unload the wagon, but Mr. Bedkin headed toward the slave women who had jumped up the moment they had spotted him. He strode over to them, slapping his palm with his riding crop. Hannah cringed as he poked Camartha sharply in the middle of her back and rapped Liddie and Daisy on their arms and legs. Evie had scurried away, before he could reach her. He pointed to the new wagonload and told them to get moving. Hannah could not hear his exact words, but she could tell by his angry posture and gestures that his words, as well as his whip, were cruel.

Evie was never whipped and seldom punished at Hart's Tavern, as most slaves were, although she had felt sharp blows from Mrs. Hewitt's thimble in the kitchen when Mrs. Hewitt was not happy with something. At that moment Hannah said a prayer, thanking God that she was not born a slave.

# Chapter Fourteen

Peter Hart was a strong but a lonely man since his wife of ten years had died. Because her death weighed so heavily on his mind and because he was left alone with so much work to do, he seldom smiled. He did his best to run the inn, but now with Thomas in Boston, it was all he could do to manage things.

Brewing the ale was a time consuming job, causing him to neglect the needed repairs and upkeep of the inn, not to mention the care and feeding of guests. Even more worrisome was the knowledge that at any time British soldiers could demand to be quartered. What would he do when there was a pounding on the door, and they demanded to be fed and given rooms? Where would he put them? Any rooms they occupied would take the place of paying guests. Peter Hart dreaded the day this would happen, but he knew it would come. But his biggest worry was what would become of Hannah if anything happened to him.

Hart's Tavern was one of the meeting places for the Committees of Correspondence, a secret network of messengers who kept the Sons of Liberty informed of the actions and movements of the British troops. Among the guests who came and went from Harts Tavern to Boston and back were informants who passed him messages that he, in turn, delivered to the Sons of Liberty in New Kensington and beyond. Peter Hart had been meeting secretly in town, in a room behind the print shop, with other men who were bracing for what they believed would be a British attack. Long Island was valuable and vulnerable – an important strategic location for both sides. Indeed, Peter Hart believed that war was inevitable, and he would fight for the Patriots, if necessary.

Hannah did not know of her father's secret, or that Thomas was part of it.

Now on this early October morning he stopped brooding for a moment and drew his attention to the task at hand. He ran a damp cloth across the rough bar and called for Evie.

"Did you prepare the lunch?" he asked sternly, when she stood before him. It was Saturday and he was expecting new arrivals. He had to go to town to speak to Hiram McDowell at the news office about the next meeting.

"Yes, Sir," Evie replied, looking down.

"Well, what is it?" said Peter, trying to keep the exasperation out of his voice.

"Beef pies and corn."

Peter looked at the lass and his impatience dissolved. She was not more than a child herself, though he did not know her age, nor did she. Maybe he could afford to get another slave, a young, strong man to help him with the barn and animals – one who would not run away, the way Jed Shaw's slave had done the week before. Peter would treat the slave better than Shaw had, so he wouldn't run away. Yes, he needed another hand around here.

While Evie finished making the lunch, Peter left the inn to go to the barn to check the horses and wagon. He had told Hannah he would take her with him to town in the afternoon. He had been away a lot at his meetings, and Thomas had not been home in weeks. Peter felt he had been neglecting Hannah. Today he wanted to show her some attention, maybe buy her some sweets or some other small treat. Night after night he saw his daughter writing by candlelight, alone in her room. He knew she must be as lonely for her mother as he was.

He walked to the two horse stalls and gave Badger a pat. He looked at the horse's right leg, which had been lame for a few days. Better to give it another day. He harnessed up the little mare, Honeycomb, Hannah's horse. She would pull the wagon today.

That afternoon Hannah and her father rode into town. Hannah was enjoying herself immensely, because this was something they rarely did. Work always took up all their time, but today Peter Hart had turned the keys over to Mr. And Mrs. Hewitt leaving everything in their charge. Hannah smiled at the idea of someone stopping at the inn and having to deal with Mrs. Hewitt. Let's see what Mrs. Hewitt would do about serving lunch!

Hannah chattered away while her father said little. Soon the horse and wagon were tethered at the trough in front of the press office. Peter said, "I want to talk to Mr. McDowell for a few minutes. I'll look for you outside." So Hannah walked along Main Street, stopping at shops along the way, and greeting people she knew. She passed Mr. And Mrs. Squires, but Adeline was not with them.

"Good afternoon, Mrs. Squires," said Hannah, bobbing a curtsey. Is Adeline not well?"

Mrs. Squire's pretty brow wrinkled in a frown. "Good day to you, too," she said. "Nay, Adeline is not well. She is at home now, wrapped in a blanket, working a little on her sampler. If she is not better tomorrow I must send for Dr. Myers."

"Please send Adeline my greetings," said Hannah politely. No mention was made of visiting Adeline, although Hannah longed to do so. She had not seen her friend in weeks, and had much to tell her. But contagion was a real threat, and there was no cure for many of the ailments that plagued the citizens of New Kensington. Mr. And Mrs. Squires nodded and moved on. Undoubtedly they understood.

In the center of town was the latest broadsheet, tacked to a tree. Reading it was Miss Violet White. Hannah ran to her teacher. She had not been to school in two weeks because she had been so busy with the harvest and ale making.

"Miss White! Good afternoon. I am sorry I have not been to school. I have been reading at home, though, and writing letters by candlelight." Hannah's words rushed on until she realized with embarrassment that her teacher had not said a word, but had just stood politely and smiled at her enthusiastic pupil. Finally, when Hannah took a breath, Miss White held out her hand to Peter Hart, who had walked up from the press office to join them.

"How do you do. I am Violet White, Hannah's teacher. I do not believe we have met."

Peter Hart took Miss White's hand in a firm handshake. He regarded with interest this young British woman who had come to New Kensington to become the schoolmistress. He admired her fair skin and brilliant blue eyes. Her hands were soft and white, and her thick russet hair, piled on top of her head was beautiful. The quality of the fabric in her clothing was superior to any he had seen in New Kensington. Why did she come here? He wondered. Judging from her appearance she was not a woman who was accustomed to doing work of any kind. He thought about how much Clara would have loved a dress like the pale blue silk one Miss White wore.

"Is there anything of interest in today's news?" he asked, gesturing toward the broadsheet, but not taking his eyes off Miss White.

"The soldiers have started to increase in number around these parts," she replied.

How unusual, thought Peter, for a woman to show an interest in soldiers!

"What do you make of it?" she asked.

"I suspect an increase of troops could indicate some planned action," said Peter carefully. Should he trust this young woman?

"I see," she said, and then turned to Hannah, who had been observing this conversation between her father and Miss White with great interest.

"Do not worry about missing school," she said. "Hessian soldiers have taken over the schoolhouse. They have been using it as a kind of way station. They have unloaded their supplies there. I think some of them even sleep there, so I have abandoned the place for the time being. I have asked Mrs. Braithwaite if I can conduct classes in her parlor one or two days a week. Bea could attend too. It would be good for her. What do you think, Hannah?"

"Oh, yes, Miss White, I think that is a wonderful idea!"

Peter Hart smiled at his daughter's enthusiasm. He was proud of how bright and curious she was. Many girls around New Kensington could not read at all, and spent all their time embroidering and drawing. He felt a pang of guilt when he thought about how much work the child did – a burden far beyond her years – and without a mother to guide her.

With secret pride Peter Hart knew that both of his children were brighter than most others. When Thomas asked to go to Harvard College in Boston to study law, Peter immediately agreed, not worrying about who would run the inn. When Harvard College cancelled classes on May 1st, when the soldiers moved in, Thomas had chosen to stay in Boston, working with a new law firm, and befriending several of the Sons of Liberty. He was instrumental in getting messages to the Committees of Correspondence, to communicate news to the towns of Massachusetts and other colonies.

Thomas often went to Faneuil Hall, Boston's political focal point, where meetings were held. The first meeting he attended was in protest of the tea tax, where the people voted to prevent the unloading of British tea. Thomas said that that meeting, as well as those that followed, were tumultuous and exciting. Peter realized how much he missed Thomas. His son was becoming part of the Boston political scene, and was gradually drifting away from Hart's Tavern and New Kensington. Ah, yes, Peter had much to worry about.

Again, lost in his thoughts, he suddenly realized he had been staring at Miss White. Embarrassed, he nodded towards Hannah and said it was time to go.

"Please, Miss White. Won't you come visit us at the inn?"

"Yes, indeed, please do," added Peter, touching the brim of his tricorn hat.

Little did they know how portentous those words were.

# Chapter Fifteen

On Sunday Hannah went to church. There she met Mrs. Squires again, who said Adeline was feeling better, and perhaps Hannah could visit in a day or two. So on Tuesday, Hannah rode Honeycomb to town and went to visit Adeline.

After tethering the little mare to the hitching post Hannah walked up the steps of the Squire's fine house that stood in the center of Main Street. Hannah rapped lightly with the lion's head doorknocker. After a moment or two a slave wearing a spotless white apron and a scarf tied around her head opened the door. "Hello, Betty. Is Adeline feeling better today? May I come in?" asked Hannah.

"Yes, Miss," said Betty, opening the door wider. Hannah heard music coming from the parlor and followed the sound. There she saw her friend. Adeline sat prettily at the pianoforte, her long hair tied up with a pink ribbon at the top of her head, her dainty feet clad in kidskin boots. She looked thin and pale as she sat playing an *étude* by Mozart.

When she finished playing the little piece Hannah clapped. "Dear Adeline, you do play so beautifully. Has Miss White heard you play?"

Adeline turned to her friend. Her eyes looked large, her cheeks hollow. "No. I have not seen Miss White in more than a month."

"But now our classes will be in Mrs. Braithwaite's parlor, where there is a harpsichord, I am told. The Hessians have taken over the schoolhouse."

"The Hessians! I am so bored with all this talk of war and Redcoats and Hessians."

"Yes, but Adeline, you must be aware. They say a battle like none before will take place nearby." Hannah looked over her shoulder, as if someone might have overheard her comment. "The Redcoats are taking over New Kensington. Father says that Mr. William Floyd has moved his entire family from his big estate to Connecticut. The Floyd Estate is not far from here."

Adeline yawned. "Father told me that we, too, may move to Connecticut until this whole thing blows over, and the so-called Patriots come to their senses. I hear there is a school for young ladies there. There is dancing, I'm told, and more than one teacher, and I shall learn French. In two years I am to come out into society."

"Adeline! There is a war on! The colonies are trying to be free from England! How can you worry about coming out into society?"

"My father says we are Tories. If things do not improve, we shall all go back to England."

Hannah knew that many families were going back, but she also knew her father and Thomas were devout Patriots and would never leave Hart's Tavern. This was their home, come what may. Adeline's complacency worried Hannah. She felt Adeline did not realize how serious the situation was.

Betty appeared with a tray and set it down on the table without a word, bobbed a small curtsey, and left the room. On the tray were small sandwiches of egg and cucumber, glasses of cider and a plate of cookies.

Hannah looked around the fine room. Its tall ceilings were painted a pale gray-green, with white decorative moldings. A chandelier with bright crystal prisms caught the sunlight and sent fragments of rainbow colors dancing all over the walls. The mahogany furniture with its substantial arms and legs was so different from the hand-hewn chairs and tables of the inn. A beautiful woven Persian carpet covered most of the floor. Hannah loved to look at its intricate designs. But on the wall, almost spoiling the elegance of the room, a portrait of an old man glowered down at them. It was well painted, but the face looked cruel. His thick, tightly curled white wig did nothing to soften the stern face.

"This is such a lovely room, Adeline. Won't you miss it if you go to Connecticut?"

Adeline shrugged her thin shoulders. "I suppose. I never thought about it. I guess the idea of going away is something I perceive to take place in the future."

"Who is the man in that picture?" asked Hannah, pointing.

"That is my grandfather, Sir Bronwell Squires. He was a landholder in England. He glowers terribly, but I understand he was actually a kind man. The problem was that he had no teeth!"

The two girls giggled at the idea, despite themselves. It was sinful to laugh at or mock anyone, but the idea that the old man's dour face might be brightened by a toothless smile amused them both. Hannah hoped that Sir Bronwell would have understood.

"I shall miss you if you go to Connecticut," Hannah said at last, when the sandwiches were gone.

"Yes, I shall miss you as well. We must write. Which reminds me, how is your brother, Thomas? Do you receive letters from him?"

"I have not lately, but we have received word that he is well. I do try to write to him often. The post is extremely slow these days."

"Please tell him I send my regards the next time you write."

"I certainly will, Adeline. Thank you for asking about my brother."

Mrs. Squires appeared in the doorway.

"Girls, we have a visitor," she said, indicating Miss White, who stood beside her. Both girls ran over and grasped their teacher's hands.

"Are you feeling better Adeline?" asked Miss White in her refined accent. "I am hoping you will be able to join our classes in Mrs. Braithwaite's parlor."

Hannah said, "I was just telling Adeline, Miss White, that you should hear her play the piano forte. She plays ever so beautifully."

"I would like that indeed." Miss White took off her bonnet and shawl, and handed them to Betty. I shall sit here. Perhaps you will play something for me."

"Would you like a cup of herbal tea?" asked Mrs. Squires.

"Yes, that would be lovely."

So Hannah and Adeline, her mother and Miss White spent a pleasant hour or two together in the parlor. It was the last time they would be able to do so, for within the next few weeks things rapidly changed in the town of New Kensington. A few days after Hannah's visit the Redcoats moved into the Squires house, and Adeline and her family left for Connecticut. Hannah never got to say good-bye.

Hannah wrote to Thomas:

*Dear Thomas,*

*The Hessians have taken over the schoolhouse and the Redcoats have moved into the Quaker meeting house as well as the Squires' home. Adeline and her parents have moved to Connecticut. Father says they dare not take over the Church because it is the Church of England, after all, and t'would be an affront against God. Is it worth the fight, dear brother? Things were peaceful here until all this talk of war.*

*Our school term has been erratic because Miss White can no longer hold classes on a daily basis. We are meeting in Mrs. Braithwaite's parlor on Tuesdays and Thursdays. She takes the younger pupils on Wednesdays. The number of students has dwindled, however.*

*Fortunately, the ale is made and the fields are cleared. Father burned away the brush today, which sent a cloud of smoke skywards, but, just as Father predicted, it rained during the night and the fire was out by morning.*

*I hope you are well, dear brother, and that you will come home soon. The last time I saw Adeline she said to send her regards. I pray that you remain safe.*

*Your sister,*
*Hannah Wainwright Hart*

Hannah sighed as she put down her quill, inserted her letter into an envelope, and held a stick of sealing wax to the candle flame. A large drop of blood red wax dropped onto the envelope. Hannah pressed the seal into it. The seal was a heart within the shape of a pentagram – the family symbol for Hart's Tavern. How hard her father worked to keep it going! It was only a matter of time before the Redcoats or Hessians would appear at the door. Not even Mrs. Hewitt would be able to hold them at bay.

Hannah prayed, "Dear God, please let this war end. Let things go back to the way they were." But deep down Hannah knew things could never go back to the way they were. She was growing older. Her mother was gone forever. Nothing ever stays the same.

Suddenly, her white cat Muffin jumped into her lap, purring madly. Hannah stroked her and smiled. Muffin was trying to cheer her up, she thought.

"It's all right, Puss," she said. "We'll get through this. We always have."

# Chapter Sixteen

Miss Violet White put her students' hornbooks on the desk in her small bedroom. She would check these later. Right now she wanted to go to town, despite the fact that it was raining, to mail a letter to her father and one to Dr. Benjamin Franklin. She also wanted to read the latest broadsheets.

She opened the larger of her two trunks and removed an umbrella. It was a large, unwieldy contraption, but she loved it because it was a gift from her father. The first one she had ever seen had belonged to Dr. Franklin. She wrapped her shawl around her shoulders and went downstairs.

"Good morning, Mrs. Braithwaite," she said to the woman dressed in black who sat sewing in the parlor. "Good morning, Bea," she said to the young girl who was sitting beside her mother.

Classes had met only sporadically in the parlor the last few weeks, since the Hessians had taken over the schoolhouse. They had placed planks across the desks, covering them with straw mattresses and blankets to make rough beds. Violet had gone back to the schoolhouse once to retrieve some of her belongings. The men had laughed and were rude. Violet thought she might never return.

She ventured out into the rainy street, walking on the crushed oyster shells that formed the pavement, and avoiding the muddy ruts that were carved into the road by the horses and wagons. She was the only one who carried an umbrella.

Few people were out in the blustery weather. Those who passed by nodded in greeting, and some of them stared. Violet knew that when the first umbrellas were used in the colonies their owners were criticized for acting in defiance of God. Umbrella critics said that God had created the rain, and that umbrellas defied Him. As the tall church came into view, Violet remembered one rainy Sunday when she had shown the umbrella to her student, Hannah Hart. Hannah had asked why, if God gave humans brains to invent things like umbrellas, He felt that the inventors defied Him? Violet assured her that the umbrella-critics were mistaken. Violet smiled at the memory. Sometimes she, too, questioned the authority and correctness of the Church and its teachings, just as the colonists were now questioning the authority of the British government. Unlike Violet, however, the colonists were not silent in their questioning.

Violet ducked into the post office, which was located in a corner of the dry goods shop. She shook out the umbrella and left it standing on the porch.

"Good morning, Miss Fisk," she said to the gray-haired, dour-looking woman who ran the store. "I'd like to post this."

"To Philadelphia? Mail won't go out until we have enough to make it worth the trip," said Miss Fisk with a sniff. "And one to England?" Her voice trailed off, and she shook her head. "May never get there, with the blockade and all."

"Please try," replied Violet, smiling. "Now I'll look around a bit. Thank you, Miss Fisk."

Violet studied the shelves along the walls of the narrow shop, where pins and yarn, bolts of fabric, ribbons and the like were stocked. She noticed a stack of five baskets in the corner. She lifted the top one and held it at arm's length. It was extremely tightly woven of thick, greenish-yellow grasses, very smooth to the touch. Violet had never seen anything like it. It was not like the common, rough baskets in daily use in the market.

"Where did you get these?" she asked. "I've not seen anything like them in here before."

"An Indian brought them in last week," said Miss Fisk. "She traded them for some wool to weave a blanket. She'll be needing it for her baby."

"They are lovely. I'll buy one," said Violet, opening her drawstring purse. She knew she could use the basket as a "catch all" in her crowded room. She also purchased a thimble – somehow she had lost hers – then said good day to Miss Fisk and left the shop.

The sky was a bit brighter when she stepped onto the porch. The wind had picked up, whipping her skirts around her. Violet closed the umbrella and walked the short distance to the print shop, where she saw a small group of people gathered around the latest broadsheet. She read an advertisement in the middle of the page:

*For Sale. Two Negroes, both in good health.*

*Strong male who knows blacksmithing.*

*Female is good cook and seamstress.*

Slavery. Violet abhorred the idea. Back home in England slavery had been officially abolished in 1772. Her family had never owned any slaves. They had servants who could come and go as they wished, although the servants her father employed rarely left. Violet believed that one of the newest servants her father had employed had been a slave. Violet did not even remember what she looked like.

A few days later, Violet looked out the window of her little room and could hardly believe what she saw. There, walking down the main street, were Miss Fisk, Mrs. Bedkin, wife of the vintner, and her own landlady, Mrs. Braithwaite, all carrying their spinning wheels! Where were they going? She wondered. The spinning wheels were big, cumbersome things that caught on the women's long skirts as they trudged down the street. Following along were half-dozen female slaves, bearing bundles on their arms and balanced on top of their heads. Violet patted her hair into place, grabbed her shawl, and ran downstairs to satisfy her curiosity. What in the world were these women doing?

Sitting at the table alone was Bea, dressed all in black, as usual.

"Where is your mother going with her spinning wheel?" asked Violet.

Bea regarded her blankly. Violet repeated, "Where is your mother going?"

"To the church," said Bea finally in her flat voice.

Violet could not contain her curiosity. Flinging her shawl over her shoulders, she gathered up her skirts and ran down the street to catch up with them.

"Hello!" she shouted. The women turned and stopped. She caught up to them, somewhat breathless, and fell into step with Mrs. Braithwaite. "May I join you? What is this all about, if I may ask?"

"We are headed to the church," Mrs. Braithwaite replied. "There we will have a spinning circle. Some ladies from the next town will be joining us. Would you like to come?"

"Of course!" said Violet. She never turned down an opportunity for a new experience. The sight of these respectable women, along with their retinue of slaves, all carrying bundles of flax and the cumbersome spinning wheels was a sight to behold. The group stopped to rest here and there along the road, and bystanders would wave to them. A group of Redcoats hooted as they passed by, mimicking their gait.

"Pay no mind to them," said the dour Miss Fisk, who turned to Violet. "I can't imagine why you would be interested in joining our circle," she said, eyeing her up and down. Violet suddenly realized that her emerald green silk dress and her brocaded shawl were nothing like the humble, homespun garments worn by these women.

"A spinning circle?" Violet said. "Of course I want to participate!" She ignored Miss Fisk's sniff and turned again to her landlady. "Would Bea enjoy a spinning circle, Mrs. Braithwaite?" Ever since she moved into her room in the boarding house Violet had tried to reach out to the quiet and withdrawn girl, who was so different from Hannah Hart and Adeline Squires, now gone to Connecticut. She doubted that Bea even knew the alphabet, but she suspected that she was not as simple minded as people thought."

"I think not," said Mrs. Braithwaite. "This is not something Bea could do."

Violet did not say so, but she disagreed. Surely the poor girl would enjoy some company and would benefit from engaging in a productive activity! Violet wondered again what was the matter with the girl.

At last the church came into view, and the women lugged the spinning wheels through the doors and into the small anteroom that was Reverend Windsor's study. The women set the wheels down in the crowded little room along with the bundles of flax and old fabrics that would be unraveled and re-used. Soon the wheels were whirring away. The slaves Liddie, Camartha and Daisy pushed the treadles and guided the yarn through the spindles as the carded flax was spun into yarn.

Meanwhile, about twenty women were assembling in the main church. Violet joined them, suddenly realizing that the purpose of the gathering might not be only to spin. She sat near the aisle in the second pew.

A small, white-haired woman in a plain, homespun frock walked to the front of the church, and faced the others. Violet did not recognize her. A hush fell over the room as the woman began to speak. Her strong voice and ramrod posture overcame her diminutive size, giving the impression that she was one to be heard. "Good morning," she said. "I see some new faces and we welcome you to our meeting of the Daughters of Liberty, most of us being housewives, others not, but all of us women of work and commitment to the Patriot cause. My name is Polly Jewell. We gather here to discuss our cause and to spin and knit. We have agreed to drink no tea and to wear no garments of foreign make."

Some of the women turned to Violet. Suddenly she felt ashamed of her beautiful green silk dress. But, she reasoned, she was English and she had brought this clothing with her. She had purchased the dress before she had even considered coming to the New World, before she had had the conversation in her bedroom with her stepmother, Catherine. She looked around at the group of earnest women, some of them holding babies. Catherine's baby would be born just two months from now. Would she ever see her little step-sibling? As Violet wondered about these things she realized that she was feeling less and less British since she had come to live in New Kensington. But was she ready to commit to the cause of the Patriots? Was she not a loyal subject of King George III? Her father was not a political man, yet how would he feel about his daughter sympathizing with the colonists?

Yet Violet believed these people were justified in their resentment of the crown, and their desire for freedom from the King's rule. After all, they lived so far away from him. They were developing a country of their own. At that moment, Violet believed she would never permanently return to England.

She drew her attention once again to Polly Jewell, who was saying, "We are in the midst of an invasion of sorts – the billeting of British soldiers and officers in our town. They have already taken over the schoolhouse." Polly nodded at Violet, apparently aware that she was the teacher. "They also have taken over the Quaker Meeting house in Melancholy Hollow. As more troops march east from Brooklyn, they will move into our churches and homes." She stopped speaking and made eye contact with each of the women. Then she said in her steely voice, "When the officer in the red coat appears at your door, he is not making a request. He is issuing an order. The soldiers will demand food, livestock and fuel. They will take the best rooms for themselves. You will be compelled to provide blankets and soap, candles and ale. They will take grain for their horses, and they will help themselves to your hogs and poultry. Will you be ready for this? I assure, you, ladies, they will come, and they will take over your homes, whether or not you are ready."

"What can we do?" asked Mrs. Braithwaite in a trembling voice.

Polly continued, "The occupation is unavoidable. As I see it, there are only two choices: stay or leave. Several families, both Tory and Patriot, have fled to Connecticut. The William Floyd family has left their vast estate and the Redcoats have taken over the entire place. I have heard that the soldiers have allowed their horses to roam through the rooms of the house. They have chopped down a huge section of the orchard, destroyed the fences along with acres of timber. I do not like to list the many atrocities that have occurred there. Other families, right here in New Kensington, have left as well. I would say that moving to Connecticut is one option. It seems to be relatively safe there."

A hum of worried voices spread throughout the room as the women reacted to Polly's words. Violet sensed fear, but also determination. Again Polly's voice rose above the rest and again there was silence. "The other option is to stay," she said. "If you stay, you stand a better chance of protecting your property, your stores, and your livestock. It will not be easy. And there are our children to consider."

Eyes turned to a young mother who sat at the back of the group, holding an infant to her breast. Violet remembered the looks on the faces of the Hessians and the Redcoats as they pushed their way into the schoolhouse. Who would protect the innocent children from them? She felt her pulse start to race and her face grow hot with anger. Polly raised her hand to quiet the group. Then Miss Fisk stood up. "I say we resist!" she said. "Don't make it easy for them!"

A clamor of voices agreed. "Yes! I say we stay and stand firm! Hide what you can. Don't give in if you can help it. Inform others! Stand strong!"

Violet could imagine the Redcoats and Hessians invading Miss Fisk's dry goods shop, carelessly tossing her carefully arranged items, helping themselves to whatever they wanted. Violet had a vision of their horses trotting around in the store, the way they did at the Floyd Estate. No wonder Miss Fisk was so agitated! Violet was amazed at the energy she felt in the room. It was like the electricity Ben Franklin had discovered!

At the end of the meeting Violet got up along with the others and made her way into Reverend Windsor's study. The spinning wheels were still going at top speed. Camartha was unraveling old brown silk stockings and crimson chair covers and spinning the threads onto spools. These colors would be woven into striped fabrics. The New Kensington Daughters of Liberty sat down among their slaves and began their own needlework.

Violet wondered what would become of Camartha, Liddie, Evie, Daisy, Betty, and all the other slaves when the Redcoats took over. Where would they go? Violet pondered their fate as well as her own as she quietly closed the door and left the church.

Two days after the meeting of the Daughters of Liberty Violet came downstairs to find Bea sitting alone in the parlor. She was looking out the window with her back turned to Violet. "Good morning, Bea," said Violet. Bea did not turn.

"Good morning!" Violet repeated, this time more loudly. Still Bea did not respond. Violet then clapped her hands sharply. Still no response. Gradually Violet made her way to the window, where Bea was sitting, clapping her hands all the way. Finally Violet stood directly behind Bea and clapped her hands sharply behind her head. Finally, Bea turned to face her, smiling her blank smile.

She is nearly deaf! Violet realized with a rush of sympathy for the girl. She pulled over a stool and sat beside her. "Can you hear me now Bea?" She said the words in a loud voice, slowly and clearly. Bea nodded her head. "Do you know that you have a hearing problem?" she asked. Again, Bea nodded. Suddenly Violet realized that Bea was reading her lips. Violet wondered how much hearing Bea possessed. Would a doctor be able to tell? She wished her father could examine her. As Violet had suspected, Bea was not simple minded at all, but rather she was nearly deaf. She asked Bea a question in the same strong, clear voice." Do you know how to read?"

Bea responded with a smile. "A little," she said. "But I have no books." Her voice was strangely flat and she did not pronounce the endings of her words.

"Would you like to read with me sometimes?" asked Violet, growing excited at the prospect of helping this girl.

Bea nodded her head vigorously and smiled. Violet got up and went back to her room. She pulled out a thin volume from her trunk, a book of Bible verses. She brought it downstairs and handed it to Bea, who opened it carefully. "Can you read this?" asked Violet.

"Bea was able to read only the simplest sentences. Her voice was flat and expressionless, but there was joy on her face. "Would you like to join my classes and learn to read?" asked Violet.

"Oh, yes, Miss White," said Bea, with a smile, the first Violet had ever seen emanating from this girl. "I would like to do many things."

Violet decided that as soon as Mrs. Braithwaite got home she would talk to her about Bea. Surely, she had noticed her deafness. Perhaps she could not accept the girl's condition. Perhaps she believed that Bea was not smart. But Violet was convinced that Bea could learn, just like the other students. She decided to go to meet Dr. Myers. She wanted to get to know him anyway; she had never had a health problem, thank God, but it would be wise to get to know him now. She would tell him about her father and Ben Franklin. She wanted to discuss the smallpox epidemic that was raging through New England, and the typhoid and typhus that were rampant. Did he have any cures, or preventions, she wondered?

But first she would need a plan for when the soldiers took over the boarding house, as they inevitably would. It was only a matter of time. She decided that when that time came she would go to Hart's Tavern.

# Chapter Seventeen

One evening in late September, Goody stood outside her doorway and watched the moon rise over the meadow. It was one of her favorite sights. Tonight the Full Harvest Moon was as golden as a ripe melon on the horizon of the deep indigo sky. Goody knew the names of all the moons, according to local Indian lore, from the Full Wolf Moon of January, when hungry wolves howl outside the native villages, to the Long Nights Moon of December. A light breeze drifted out of the southwest carrying with it the scent of the sea. Goody suddenly wondered about the young Indian woman who never came back with the sick child. This Indian had had the scent of the sea about her.

With some difficulty Goody walked to her rocker on the porch and sat down. She decided to enjoy the view a bit longer, until the evening grew cold. One of her cats strolled around her legs until it finally jumped into her lap and purred as Goody's gnarled old hands stroked her back. Goody knew that people believed she was an eccentric hermit. Some even called her a witch. She had many secrets, and no one really knew the truth about her.

Goody's Christian name was Grace Alice Cooper. She grew up in Boston to a Tory family, in a fine house near the old North Church. Grace was taught to curtsey and dance the minuet, and make polite conversation. She was expected to learn to play the pianoforte and do embroidery. But Grace was a headstrong and willful girl. She longed to be outdoors, not sitting inside with her embroidery hoop. She loved to run through Boston Common, letting her wild red hair tumble around her shoulders. She was attracted to all living things, and often brought home doves and butterflies. She adored dogs, cats and horses, but the idea of a cat or a dog in the house was unheard of, and horses stayed in the stables until harnessed to the carriage.

Grace despised Boston society life and decided to set out on her own. When she was eighteen she packed a small bag and left town, heading for the New York colony. When she arrived in Brooklyn she headed east, to the south shore of Long Island.

One day she came to New Kensington on the stagecoach to stop for a few days at Hart's Tavern, when Peter Hart's grandfather was the proprietor. Three days later a young Secatogue Indian knocked upon the door and asked if he might use the well for a drink of water. He was the handsomest man Grace had ever seen. She felt compelled to follow him outside to the well. He spoke English. Grace thought he was intelligent and wonderful. He came back to the inn the next day, and the day after that. They began to keep company. Keme (his name meant *thunder* in the Algonquin language) told her about his people, his animals, and his hunting and fishing prowess. He showed her the belts of white and purple wampum he owned. One day he took her to the edge of the Great Bay. He took her hand, placed a large, black pearl into her palm, and asked her to become his wife. Grace accepted immediately. Her journey from Boston would end in New Kensington, where her new life would begin. Soon she was expecting a child.

How she loved her fine, strong husband! They built their cottage together, and planned their future. They wanted to start a farm and live simply. But their happiness did not last. Like many of his tribe, Keme succumbed to disease, as did their child, a baby boy. Grace kept her grief inside her. She felt as if her heart had turned to stone.

As years went by, Grace made it her business to learn all she could about healing methods, herbs, poultices, and even spells. People started calling her Goody Garlicke because of her talents with plants. Years went by, and Grace Alice Cooper was forgotten. Goody Garlicke had taken her place. She lived alone, with her cats and dogs, earning a little by selling her cures to those who came to her cottage. Mostly, though, she kept to herself.

Goody looked up as a wisp of breeze drifted by. She saw that in the distance the tall reeds swayed beside the road alongside the marsh. The full moon hung over the scene, as if in anticipation.

Suddenly there appeared a horse and rider, galloping west. Few travelers appeared on this rough trail. Most of them took the main road through town. Goody wondered who this traveler could be.

She got up from her chair and went into the cottage. She reached between some jars on the shelf by the door and took out a leather-bound journal, pen and ink. Goody made a practice of writing down what she observed. It gave her something to do and made sense of her days. The last entry in her journal was a notation of Wyanjoy's visit.

Now she sat at her table, dipped the pen into the inkwell and wrote in her large, spidery handwriting, *September 28, 1775. Shortly after moonrise a lone rider passed by.* Then she got up from her chair and put the journal back in its place on the shelf.

# Chapter Eighteen

The wind roared and the rain poured in a whirlwind unlike any Hannah had seen or heard before. Branches and sticks flew, striking at the windows. The wind reverberated through the eaves and walls, causing the candles to flicker and sparks to fly out of the fireplace. As if unaware of the tempest, Evie sat on a stool in a corner, her knitting on her lap, and Hannah walked around the small dining room, filling the guests' glasses and listening to their talk.

"When is this infernal weather going to end?" complained Mrs. Hewitt, flinging her fox tails around her shoulders. She gripped a tankard of ale with two hands and downed it in a few gulps.

"'Tis one of the storms that comes up from the southeast this time of year," said Peter Hart from the bar. He poured two more tankards of ale and brought them to her table. Mrs. Hewitt frowned in disapproval as her husband accepted his gratefully. Peter Hart observed them with some amusement. He wondered if they were happy together, as he had been with Clara. He closed his eyes, listening to the howl of the wind, and he remembered another stormy night, years ago, when Clara had sat at her spinning wheel, where Evie now sat. He could almost see her, in her plain brown frock, her eyes merry and a song on her lips. Clara was a woman of many talents, and he had loved her with all his heart.

She had always been strong and healthy, working side by side with him in the inn and outdoors. She loved riding horses and going for long walks along the shore of the Great Bay. But one day she didn't seem herself. By nightfall she burned with fever and Peter was frightened. He sent for Dr. Myers, who said she was suffering from illness caused by bad blood. Peter shuddered at the memory of Clara, lying on the bed, dressed in her white nightgown, as Dr. Myers applied leeches to her arms to bleed her. During the next few days Clara continued to do poorly, becoming even more pale and weak. Dr. Myers said she needed to be bled more, and so it was done, plus a thick poultice was applied to her chest and more quilts and blankets were piled on her to cause the fever to break. Yet nothing helped. And so it came to be that after this short illness, Clara was taken from Peter, leaving Thomas and Hannah to grow up motherless.

Their slave, Old Sally, cared for the children while Peter worked the fields and ran the inn. Hannah grew into a young woman, very much like her mother, and now Thomas was in Boston. What would Peter do when Hannah left to start a life of her own? Would he remain at the inn by himself?

But right now was the immediate, very real danger of the storm. Peter did not want to alarm his guests, but he feared the storm might bring tides that would break through the barrier beach, causing the ocean to surge into the Great Bay and flood Melancholy Hollow. It had happened once before, when he was a young lad. At that time there were few buildings in the area, but the native people had suffered greatly. Their entire village had been destroyed. He remembered them wandering through the streets of New Kensington the day after the storm, stunned and devastated. Soon after the storm came the sickness, wiping out more than half their numbers. Peter knew that along with the British the greatest enemy was disease. He prayed that the storm would subside.

Suddenly there was a pounding on the door. Hannah and Evie watched fearfully as Peter Hart hurried to open the door. A tall, drenched man entered the room. The door blew shut with a bang, causing the windows to rattle. The man put his dripping hat and coat on a peg by the door. Then he and Peter Hart disappeared into the room behind the bar, while Hannah hurried to the small kitchen to get him some food.

"Evie, come help me!" she said to the girl. Evie rose from her stool and joined Hannah. The two girls cut bread and cheese and ladled out some soup into a large wooden bowl. "Make some coffee, said Hannah."

Hannah put the food on a tray and leaned against the adjoining door to open it. Her father and the man were engaged in deep conversation.

"We haven't got much time," said the tall man. His deep voice was full of exhaustion and urgency. "The British are planning to move troops into Brooklyn within the next week. Some say a battle is inevitable. We have to warn Brewster."

"How can we do it?" asked Peter Hart, as if questioning himself. "Brewster is hiding in the coves of Melancholy Hollow. We are too well known to send someone to him. The runner could be seen and reveal Brewster's hiding places. Somehow we need to let him know about the troop movements so he can tell George Washington's informants."

Hannah cleared her throat and came into the room. She was not sure she should be hearing this conversation. She put the tray down in front of the man and bobbed a curtsey. "Coffee is coming in a minute."

Hannah knew the colonists were breaking away from England in many different ways. They no longer even drank British tea! She did not understand all of what was happening, but she believed the separation from England was like a child growing up and moving away from home. It was natural and inevitable. Hannah shuddered at the thought of what the cost of such a separation would mean. War was something people talked about. Battles were fought in places she had never seen. Thank God there had been no fighting in New Kensington, at least not yet. Hannah feared this serious young man brought worrisome news. Evie appeared with the coffee, which the man took gratefully.

"Thank you, miss, he said, smiling at Evie. Hannah noticed that his skin was almost the same color as Evie's, and that his large, dark eyes held fear. Was this the runaway slave who had been written about in the weekly broadsheets in town? She turned to Evie, who was staring at the man, as if in disbelief. Evie's hand shook as she handed him a spoon.

How did her father know this man? Hannah wondered. Suddenly it occurred to her that this man was not only a runaway slave, but a spy. It was a perfect way to cover up his comings and goings – a slave on the run.

Hannah's thoughts continued to race. If this man was a spy, then so must be her father and Thomas! This realization took her breath away. Waves of fear caused her to tremble and her heart to pound. They were taking a terrible risk! The situation was almost unbearable to contemplate.

Much later, when the storm had subsided and the man had gone, Hannah's father called her into the kitchen. "Let's go for a walk," he said. Hannah was puzzled, but said nothing. Taking her wool cloak from the peg by the door, she followed her father. The pair walked towards the meadow. The rain had stopped, but the wind still whipped around the willow trees at the edge of the hill. Hannah drew her cloak tighter around her body. Her father had never asked her to go for a walk in this manner, in such weather as this. She sensed he wanted to tell her something, and she was right.

They made their way to the big maple tree that stood on the hill, at the high point of the meadow. He father gestured toward the Great Bay, speaking animatedly. Hannah nodded in agreement, fascinated by what he said. Finally Hannah understood.

Early the next morning, when the pale sun was just filtering its weak light through the nearly leafless trees, Hannah went up the back stairs to the narrow hallway above the kitchen. At the end of the hallway was a door, fastened with a latch. Hannah opened the latch and lifted her skirts to climb the narrow stairway that led to the attic. The small room was cold, dusty and cheerless. Under the eaves of the slanting roof the space was filled with crates of bedding, tools, and other supplies. At the peak of the roof was a small window that let in a shaft of light that revealed dust motes, stirred from their sleep when Hannah had pushed open the door. The light beamed down on a brown leather trunk that sat in the corner. Hannah took a big key ring from her apron pocket and opened the trunk. She was not prepared for the reaction she had when she lifted its lid.

The sight of what lay in the trunk brought a rush of hot tears to her eyes that ran down her cheeks and chin. Sobs rose from somewhere within her and found their voice. Hannah lifted out each piece of her mother's clothing and brought it to her face. She sniffed. Was that a scent of the rose water her mother always wore, or was it just a memory she associated with the garments? There were three red petticoats and three white ones, a plain, brown homespun dress, a fancier calico dress with a little pattern of birds and flowers colored black, white and red. The last dress was her mother's best one, a blue velvet frock that she saved for special occasions. There were also two shawls and some undergarments. Hannah had not seen these things since before her mother had died. Carefully she shook out the petticoats and dresses. Perhaps she would wear them one day.

She refolded the three dresses and put them back in the trunk, but the petticoats she kept out. She took another look around the room. It was cold and drafty, but perhaps something could be done with it one day. She closed the lid of the trunk and turned the key in the lock. Grasping the petticoats she climbed down the stairs and closed the door behind her. Tomorrow she would help Evie do the laundry, and the petticoats would be washed along with everything else. Hannah would hang them carefully on the newly positioned clothesline. In this way, she would help her father, Thomas, and the Patriot cause.

# Chapter Nineteen

Hannah wrote,

*Dear Thomas,*

*How are you, my brother? I wonder if you miss us as much as we miss you. And I worry about you, Thomas. There are many comings and goings here at the inn. I shall not write about them, except to mention that Mr. and Mrs. Hewitt are helping. They are a funny pair. Mrs. Hewitt is a large woman who tolerates no nonsense. Her husband is small and quiet, and wears a dreadful wig. I am glad they help Father, but I wish you were here instead. I did not see any Redcoats today, but their presence is felt everywhere. They are quite visible in town, and everyone worries that a battle will come this way.*

*A dreadful storm passed through last evening, taking down several trees at the edge of the meadow. . .*

Hannah heard a slight sound looked up to see Evie standing in the doorway. She put down her quill.

"Yes, Evie?" she said.

"I would like to write a letter, too," said the slave.

Hannah knew that Evie could not read or write. It was unheard of for slaves to go to school, especially a girl, so what could she mean? Hannah said nothing, waiting for Evie to go on.

"I want to send a letter to New York, to a woman there who might know my sisters and brothers."

"You never told me your family was still in New York."

Evie hung her head, as if ashamed. "I'm not sure, Miss Hannah, but the other night, when that man came to see Mr.

Hart, I thought about them all night. I wonder if they are alive or dead. I want to know."

"Well, then, you must write the woman a letter. We can take it to the post office tomorrow. Do you want to send it to General Delivery in New York?"

Hannah did not want to ask Evie the names of her parents or siblings. Their African names had undoubtedly been changed, perhaps more than once if they were bought and sold several times. Slaves had only one name.

"No, not the post office," said Evie. "I want to give it to the man who came here to visit your father. I know him."

"You know him!" Hannah stared at Evie.

"Yes. I remember him from the day I was taken to New York." Once again she looked at the floor. She never discussed her past with Hannah. The only friends Evie had were slaves on the farms nearby, or in town. She and Hannah lived and worked together, but they were not sisters.

"If I tell you what I want to say, would you write it down for me, Miss Hannah?"

Hannah looked at Evie's nut-brown face and huge black eyes with their thick, curly lashes framed by her muslin mobcap. For the first time Hannah realized how pretty Evie was. She asked so little, and now this!

"Well, of course, Evie," she said. "But perhaps you should write it yourself."

"You know I cannot write," she said quietly.

"You could learn," persisted Hannah. "I could teach you."

"No, Miss Hannah. There is not time. I want to write it now."

Hannah regarded Evie in a new way. She had always taken her for granted. She was a part of the household, just like the litters of cats and Honeycomb. Now she could see that Evie had her own thoughts and feelings. This letter must be very important to her.

"All right, then," said Hannah, taking out a fresh sheet of paper from her writing box and dipping her quill into the ink. "How do you wish to start?"

Evie paused only briefly. She had memorized what she wished to say.

*Dear Miss Baker,*

*I have been wondering about my brothers and sisters whom I have not seen since I was sold in New York eight years ago. Nor my mother and father, who may be dead. I heard you are free and you care for young'uns. I was just wondering if you know my family. Their names are Kimani, Solomon and Opal. Signed Evie, slave of Peter Hart, New Kensington, New York.*

Hannah dipped her quill over and over again in the ink bottle as Evie spoke, writing rapidly, changing a word here and there, hoping to make Evie's meaning clear. How did Evie know this woman, wondered Hannah. Who was she? Would this letter ever find its way into her hands? She wondered if Miss Baker could read. If so, that would be quite remarkable. Would Evie ever get a reply? Hannah was doubtful.

Evie's words disturbed Hannah. Although she knew Evie had brothers and sisters, she had never known their names. That's just the way it was with slaves. But now she wondered how she would she feel if she were never to see Thomas again. The idea was unthinkable. She felt a pang of sympathy for the young woman standing before her, as well as guilt. She had spent years of her childhood with Evie, side by side, and never really knew her.

"Is there anything else you would like to say?" she asked.

"No, Miss Hannah. That is all."

"How do you want me to address the envelope?" she asked.

Evie thought a minute, and then said, "To Miss Cleta Baker, Freed Slave and Cake Baker. New York City." Hannah wrote the address carefully, and put Hart's Tavern, New Kensington, as the return address.

Evie held out her hand for the letter, examining it with satisfaction. The ink was dry. "Thank you, Miss Hannah," she said.

That night Evie buried her head in her pillow and sobbed. She had been doing this almost every night since the tall, dark man had come to the inn that stormy night. She knew he was the runaway slave of Jed Shaw. It was only a matter of time before he would be returned to his master, beaten, and put in the stocks. How could life be so cruel?

She remembered the day she was pulled away from her mother. They had been living in a crowded cabin, six or seven of them, all in one room. She did not even know where it was, but soon she was on a wagon with several others who joined them along the way. The ride was rough. She remembered how hungry and thirsty she was. When one of the older captives, a teenager named Blanchard, jumped off the wagon and tried to escape, two of the drivers ran after him into the woods and captured him. Evie and the others were held at the point of a rifle, and dared not move. The boy was dragged back, bloody from the whipping he had received for trying to run away. When he was back in the wagon he sat next to Evie. She wiped the blood from his brow with her handkerchief. He held her hand tightly and said he would free them all one day. She looked deeply into his huge eyes, and he kissed her.

After what seemed like a long time Evie remembered standing on a platform, crowded together with slaves from the wagon as well as others she did not know. There was blood on her skirt from a deep cut on her thigh where a whip had snapped, urging her to move faster. The slaves were in a city called New York.

One by one the boys and men were taken away in chains, as they were sold to the highest bidders. She remembered Blanchard being led away. For a moment they made eye contact, and Evie remembered his promise. She was one of the last to remain on the platform, being so small and skinny, along with a tiny old, gray-haired woman whom nobody wanted. Suddenly Peter Hart appeared and gestured to the auctioneer. He purchased them both.

Evie knew things could have been worse. Peter Hart was a kind and quiet man, and he never beat her or old Sally, even once. But as she grew up in the household she knew in her heart that she would never feel like a member of this family. The memory of her own parents was too strong, her capture and her experience at the slave market too raw. But sometimes a flicker of memory from some distant past would cross her mind, and she would feel happy. She remembered bits of songs and poetry that she would sing when she worked outside.

When she first arrived at the inn Evie learned that Peter Hart's wife had died, and that he needed someone to take care of his two children, Thomas and Hannah. The children were strong and feisty and needed a firm hand and a kind heart. Sally became Hannah's and Evie's surrogate mother, and they grew to love her. Evie became a companion to Hannah, and as time went by, Hannah came to depend on her.

But as Hannah got older she grew apart from Evie, turning her interest to reading and books. She had little use for the finer skills girls were supposed to enjoy, like stitching samplers and embroidering linens. Mrs. Squires had offered to give Hannah lessons on the pianoforte along with her daughter, Adeline, but Hannah soon lost interest. Hannah liked to ride her horse, and run in the fields, perhaps because she was never swaddled or put on a board to prevent her from crawling. Peter Hart did not believe in these customs. Hannah and Thomas grew up free to run and move as much as they wished. Ladies of the town disapproved of Hannah's wild running and horse riding, and felt sorry for the two motherless children.

Old Sally died when Hannah was ten. Now all the heavy housework was left to Evie. She got up before dawn each day to get the fire going. She cleared ash from the coals and added pieces of bark and sticks to ignite the embers that had glowed all night. She added a few large logs, and soon the fire roared.

Once the fire was lit she went from room to room, emptying wash basins into a bucket and taking chamber pots outside to empty. With that done, she went to the barn to milk the cow and goats. She took the milk to the kitchen and poured it into pans so that the cream could rise to the top. Later she would churn the cream into butter.

Next, Evie went to the hen house to gather eggs, and to the well to haul buckets of fresh water. By then, the sun was rising, and the others in the inn would be stirring. Peter Hart and Hannah would get up, and get dressed. Peter would go to the barn before breakfast, and Hannah would join Evie to help Mrs. Hewitt prepare breakfast and serve the guests, who would assemble at the long table for a breakfast of fresh eggs and bread, perhaps with some cheese and jam, a piece of smoked fish or bacon, and hot coffee laced with chicory.

When the meal was over, Evie and Hannah cleared the table. For the rest of the day Evie continued with her chores. Depending on the season, she would tend to the hops garden, weed the vegetable garden, spin wool into yarn, knit, weave, and sew. And then there was the bedding to be aired, rooms to be cleaned, linens to be boiled and washed, and soap and candles to be made. Hannah worked too, cleaning the rooms, brushing the animals, and washing dishes. But afterwards, unlike Evie, she would go to school.

As Evie grew older, she thought continuously about her past. Vague memories of her mother and father being dragged off a ship, then the separation – the young man, Blanchard, who was whipped for trying to run away – these thoughts played over and over in her mind. Old Sally would have said a spirit was calling to her, but Evie knew otherwise. It was the voice of Freedom. Evie wanted to live her own life. She knew she was more fortunate than most to live in her small room at the back of the inn, next to the kitchen. She had enough food to eat, and was never beaten. But what was her fate? Would she ever have a child of her own? Such thoughts were dangerous for a slave. She also knew she could be sold at any time. If the soldiers in the red coats came to the inn to stay, what would happen? If she ran away, where would she go, and what would become of her?

On the night of the storm, Evie had recognized the man who came to the inn as Blanchard, the boy who had tried to run away when he was in the wagon with Evie, so many years ago. Now he was a spy for the Patriots, the runaway slave of Jed Shaw. She wondered where he was now. Evie decided she would find him and give him the letter. She figured that he must travel between New Kensington and New York City. He might know Cleta Baker. She would talk to Camartha and Liddie. They would know where he was hiding. Evie remembered the way Blanchard had kissed her goodbye. She loved him then, and she loved him now. Somehow this idea comforted her. She turned on her back, closed her eyes, and finally fell asleep.

The next morning she awoke to the sound of Mrs. Hewitt, calling her from the dining room. Evie got up from her little bed and hurried out to the kitchen.

"Where have you been?" asked Mrs. Hewitt angrily, rapping Evie sharply on the head with her thimble. "The fire is nearly out! And did I not tell you to clear these dishes last night? Put a pot of water to boil and then come back and see to it that this floor is scrubbed." She stomped off to find her husband, who would undoubtedly receive the next tongue-lashing.

Evie went into the kitchen and quickly got the water bucket to take to the well. She did not want to anger Mrs. Hewitt. There was only trouble for a slave who crossed the path of one like her. Evie's resolve suddenly grew stronger. Somehow, some day, she would be free. Some day she would have control of her own time and her own life. Was this a foolish thought?

"Oh, Lord," prayed Evie. "Let me be free. These people want to be free of the Redcoat soldiers, but they won't let us be free." Then Evie felt better and stronger. She was certain now that one day an opportunity would present itself, and she would be able to run, free. If not, she would die trying.

# Chapter Twenty

Balancing the laundry basket on her hip, Hannah walked up the hill to the highest point of the meadow, where the Great Bay came into sharp focus. The sky was brilliant blue, with no clouds. She set the basket under the big maple tree where she had rested on ale making day. Now a clothesline hung between this tree and a smaller one near the well. A few angry black crows squawked in protest, as if demanding to know why Hannah had disturbed their meadow.

Hannah took the clothes out of the basket and hung them up with wooden pins. She put the two red petticoats in the middle of the clothesline, with the other garments around them. On this clear day the petticoats would be visible from the road leading along the bay to Melancholy Hollow. They could also be seen with a spyglass by any small boat along the shore. The clothes flapped briskly in the wind.

Her father had given her instructions as to which petticoats to hang on the clothesline. One white petticoat meant no news. Two white ones meant it was time to ride and pick up a message from one of the secret meeting places of the committees of correspondence, one of which was Hart's Tavern. Hannah guessed the red petticoat signal had something to do with the movements of the Redcoats. She knew that the mysterious visitor had come to the inn to plan the signals with her father. She knew that he carried information to the east, then across the Long Island Sound to Connecticut by whaleboat. From there it was relayed to Patriots in the north. She breathed a sigh of satisfaction. She was helping the Patriots. Would it help to end the war? She picked up her basket and made her way back to the inn.

Evie was standing by the door, under the sign with the pentagon. Hannah had not discussed the signal of the petticoats with her, but she figured that Evie had noticed. The clothesline had been moved, and hanging wash had been one of her chores until Hannah had started hanging the petticoats.

"Someone is here to see you," said Evie. Her expressive dark eyes were wide and questioning. Hannah handed her the laundry basket and went into the inn. She was surprised at what she saw: there at a table sat Miss White and her father.

"Good morning, Hannah," said Miss White. She looked lovely, as usual, thought Hannah. But there was concern in her voice. Did she bring bad news?

"The boarding house has been taken over," she said simply. "Your father said I might stay here. There are Redcoats in all the rooms of Mrs. Braithwaite's home. She and Bea are sharing one room. All of the others are taken."

"I thought perhaps we could clean up the attic space and Violet could stay there," said Peter Hart. "Hannah, what do you think?"

Hannah knit her brows together. It would be wonderful to have Miss White at the inn, but the attic was cold and dusty. Still, with a little cleaning, and a brazier to keep it warm . . . and there was a tiny window to let in some light . . . yes, she thought the room could be made quite cozy.

"I will get Evie to start dusting the attic room," she said.

"Thank you so much!" said Violet White, with obvious relief. "Of course I can pay whatever is the going rate."

Just then Mrs. Hewitt came into the room. She eyed Violet White up and down with suspicion, as if to ask what nerve she had to be here in the dining room.

"Good morning," said Violet pleasantly. "I am Violet White, Hannah's teacher. I have been living at Mrs. Braithwaite's boarding house and holding classes there since the schoolhouse was taken over by Hessians. Now I am afraid the boarding house has also become occupied, so I have been forced to leave. Mr. Hart has graciously found a room for me."

Mrs. Hewitt's eyes narrowed. "We serve two meals a day. You eat what we serve," said Mrs. Hewitt in her loud voice. Hannah smiled. That was a change from the time Mrs. Hewitt complained about the mutton stew! Now she did a lot of the cooking for the inn. Hannah had to admit that Mrs. Hewitt was, indeed, a good cook, even if her demeanor was less than friendly.

By evening Evie and Hannah had cleaned the little attic room from top to bottom, while Miss White went with Mr. Hewitt to fetch her two trunks from Mrs. Braithwaite's house. Hannah wondered where to put them. Would they fit in the small space under the slanted ceiling? Evie and Hannah pushed Hannah's mother's trunk into the far corner, under the eaves, thus making room under the small window. The two trunks might fit there.

For now, the bed was just a small straw mattress on a pallet, but it was covered with two clean, thick patchwork quilts, and one of Hannah's nice feather pillows. Her father repaired a small table that had been languishing in the barn. The table now served as a desk. An extra kitchen chair completed the furnishings.

Hannah surveyed the room once more. It was ready! Suddenly she had an idea. She went down the little stairway, through the dining room, and into her own room. On her table sat a jar containing the four orange seeds Jeremy had given her. They had sprouted into tiny pale green stems. She went to the kitchen and looked around for a suitable container. Finally she settled on a small clay jug with a small chip on top. It wouldn't be missed. She took this outside to the hops garden where the soil was well worked and soft. She filled the jug with soil and brought it to her room. Then, with extreme care, she took a teaspoon and gently dug out one of the sprouted seeds. Hannah made a hole in the soil with her finger and gently pressed the little sprout into it. Would it grow in the pale light of Miss White's new room? It would be an interesting experiment to see how it fared compared to the remaining three seeds in Hannah's room. She hoped it would make Miss White happy.

Peter Hart set up a shelf on two stacks of bricks against the far wall of the dining room to hold Violet White's books. In a matter of days Miss White became a part of the household of the inn.

After dinner each evening she talked about England and her home on Craven Street. She told about her friendship with Benjamin Franklin and his amazing experiments. Sometimes she would read aloud, other times she would guide the others in their own reading. Even Mrs. Hewitt cocked an ear as she pretended to dust or clear up the tables.

Everyone joined in discussions involving the war. Hannah wondered aloud how the King felt about his colonies. Did he know about New Kensington and its people? "What is the King like, Miss White?" she asked.

Violet White frowned briefly. "I have never met him, but my father did. The King was thrown from a horse near Craven Street, and my father was called to assist. He was terribly bruised and shaken. My father insisted that he be taken home to the palace to rest, but the King and his wife had theater tickets that evening, and he had promised to take her. I would say that King George is a man of his word."

"Why does he feel he has the right to tax us?" asked Hannah.

"It is quite complicated, and I do not defend his view. But the King thinks that since we in the colonies are English citizens we must pay taxes to him."

"But there is no representation!" said Mrs. Hewitt, coming into the room.

"Yes, I know," said Miss White quietly. Once again she was torn between her love for England and her loyalty to the people here in New Kensington. They were all of the same flesh and blood. Was it really necessary to go to war over taxes? But Violet realized it was much more than that. The colonies were growing apart from their king, just as she had grown apart from her father.

# Chapter Twenty-one

The meadow seemed to extend forever. Evie looked up and saw a hawk circling overhead, then another. She shivered and hoped this was not a bad omen. She tried to walk as casually as possible, hoping that her sense of urgency would not be noticed in case anyone was watching her.

She approached the stone wall at the end of the apple orchard. Most of the apples had been picked or had fallen. Along the wall, clumps of bright goldenrod grew along with a few remaining blue chicory flowers, purple thistle, and her favorite, the golden little snapdragons known as butter and eggs. A steady wind whipped her skirts around her legs.

Finding a low spot, she climbed over the wall and dropped down. Several feet beyond the wall was the cemetery. Evie felt another chill, although the breeze was warm. How many ghosts were watching her? She wondered. She almost never came through the meadow this way, but it was the shortest route to the tiny log cabin where Camartha lived. Mr. Bedkin, the vintner, lived in the big house at the top of the hill with his wife and children. Had they seen her?

Evie picked up her skirts and ran. She couldn't be gone too long. The days were shorter now, and she had to get to Camartha's cabin and back to Hart's Tavern before it grew dark. A plan was forming in her mind, although it had not taken full shape. She was breathless by the time she reached the little house.

She banged on the door and Camartha opened it immediately. Evie stepped into the dark room. Only one small window, covered with greased paper, provided light. As her eyes adjusted to the dimness, Evie spied a man sitting at a little table in the corner. He had a hat pulled down low over his eyes. It was Blanchard. Evie had not seen him since the night of the storm. She rushed across the room and flew into his arms. They hugged in a long embrace until Camartha said, "Say what you have to say. It'll be dark soon and Blanchard must leave. I'll wait outside and watch. If you hear me talking or singing, it means someone's nearby." With that warning, Camartha left the two of them alone.

"How've you been, Blanchard?" Evie asked, taking his hands in hers.

Blanchard did not reply, but Evie could read the answer in his eyes.

"What will they do with you if you get caught?"

"I won't," he said simply.

"I want to come with you," she said.

"Not yet," he replied. "It is too soon. I'm traveling again tonight. I'll get the horse after dark and take my usual route. If I see lights on the water, I will be able to give the signal. In a few weeks, when all this is over – when the British take over Long Island – I'll be free to leave. Then you can come with me."

"How long will that be? This is too dangerous."

He shrugged. He didn't care about the danger. He knew this was his only way to escape, and to gain his freedom – his and Evie's. They would go to Canada and never come back.

Evie took the letter out of her pocket and handed it to him. "Please take this and find her," she said, pointing to the name on the envelope. "She may know my family. She may be able to help us."

Blanchard tucked the letter deep into his pocket. Then he drew Evie into his arms and kissed her fiercely.

Suddenly there was a banging on the door and Camartha came back inside. "Someone is coming," she hissed. "Now Evie, child, you git. Blanchard, you go back behind that curtain until whoever it is passes by."

Blanchard held Evie tightly. "Good-bye," he said, reluctantly releasing her to Camartha, who stood guarding the doorway.

Evie could not bear to leave him, but she pulled away and left the cabin. In the distance she could see someone approaching on horseback. As the figure drew closer she saw that it was Miss Hannah.

"Evie, I've been looking for you!" Hannah said crossly. "It is almost dark and we are not ready for dinner! The guests will be waiting! What's gotten into you?"

Evie put her head down. "I am sorry."

Hannah eyed her suspiciously. This was something new, like the letter. Evie had never been late like this before.

"Get on behind me," she said. "Honeycomb will have to take us both back home."

Hannah stretched out her hand and moved forward on the horse, making room for Evie, who hoisted herself up. Hannah nudged Honeycomb into a gallop and kept her eyes straight ahead. But Evie looked back over her shoulder at the cabin, to where Blanchard hid behind the curtain. She hoped he could see her. "Godspeed," she whispered.

She wondered if they would ever be free.

# Chapter Twenty-two

Goody sat on her small porch and watched the road. It was the fourth night in a row she had done so, because she wanted to confirm what she had suspected. She had her journal in her lap, and her heaviest shawl wrapped around her shoulders to keep away the chill breeze. It was twilight, the time of day between dogs and wolves, as her husband used to say in his own language. It is the time when you cannot tell a dog from a wolf, a friend from an enemy.

Goody watched and listened closely, as she had done the last four evenings at dusk. She smelled the air, sensing the sea salt it carried. At last she heard the faint sound of hoof beats thudding on the path alongside the marsh. She rose from her chair to get a better look. Without a doubt, it was the same shadowy horse and rider, galloping along the road beside the marsh. The rider leaned low over the horse's neck. She wondered where he came from, and what his mission was.

Goody opened her journal and wrote:

*November 18, 1775*

*At moonrise, the horseman appeared again. He rides past about every second week, always traveling east. I have not seen him on a return trip; therefore he must take the high road back, or perhaps cross over to Connecticut by boat.*

Goody closed her journal, went into her cottage and placed it back on her shelf. Something made her cross her fingers and pray for his safety.

# Chapter Twenty-three

Thomas was home! He appeared one night, all six feet of him, in the doorway. Hannah flew into his arms and held on, as if never to let him go. He was thinner, and seemed older. Could this man really be the teenager who left them only six months ago?

Peter Hart strode over to his son and also embraced him. Evie smiled and rose from her spot in the corner. Mrs. Hewitt bustled around, shooing away a stray chicken or two to make a place for Thomas at the table.

"What news, Son?" asked his father.

The two men sat down, nearly head to head. Thomas spoke quietly. "Our spies have reported an increase in British troops and movement toward Staten Island. It appears that a battle for Long Island is imminent. General Washington is preparing his men as well as he can, but the Patriots are farmers. They are not trained like the British troops."

Peter Hart eyed the shotgun that was in the corner by the fireplace. He was prepared to fire it if his home were threatened. But would he be able to use it in battle?

Thomas went on, "If the British attack Brooklyn, it is just a question of how far east they will go. Brooklyn is more than a day's journey from here on horseback. They could also come by sea. The British control all the waters around New York City. The Redcoats could capture Long Island by driving out all the Patriots. Only those loyal to the king would be left."

"We'll not leave!" said Peter.

"What about Hannah?" asked Thomas. "I understand the Squires have gone to Connecticut. They are staying near the family of William Floyd, who has left his estate in Shirley. Hannah could join them. She could be with Adeline."

Mr. and Mrs. Hewitt glanced furtively at each other, no doubt wondering what would become of them. Their own home already had been overrun. What would they do when the troops came to Hart's Tavern?

As if reading their thoughts Thomas said, "It is only a matter of time before the next battalion of troops arrives, and the inn will be occupied. All the food and ale will be taken over by the Redcoats and Hessians." He turned to Hannah. "You will be forced to bake bread for them. There will be nothing you can do."

"We'll hold firm," said Peter Hart, his mouth a tight, straight line. "We will protect our property or go down defending it. I leave it to Hannah to decide when and if she wants to go to Connecticut."

"No! I want to stay here," said Hannah. "I do not want to go to Connecticut with the Squires."

"What about you, Thomas?" asked his father quietly.

"I cannot stay long, only a few days," said Thomas.

"Why?" asked Hannah. She felt a tightness of fear in her chest.

"I must go back to Boston. The Sons of Liberty will meet to decide their next move and I must be a part of that. I will meet my friend Nathan Hale in Connecticut."

Violet White cleared her throat to make her presence known as she entered the room from the main hallway. She did not want to intrude upon the family, but the fine looking young man who had finally come home, the brother Thomas that Hannah so loved, intrigued her. The family looked up to see Violet standing there. Hannah linked arms with Thomas, and they walked across the room.

"Miss White," said Hannah smiling now. "This is Thomas."

Thomas touched the tip of his tricorn hat and nodded. "I am pleased to meet you, Miss White. I have heard a lot about you."

Violet White regarded him. His fine, brown hair was long and tied back in a ponytail. He wore a clean, white shirt, black knee breeches, and white stockings. His suede, three-quarter length coat was different from the frock coats that most men wore. It was fringed, like Indian clothing. In contrast, his black shoes had big, brass buckles. Yes, he was indeed handsome. Violet was glad he was home. She knew Hannah had missed him, and had worried about him. She extended her hand and said with a smile, "It is my pleasure to meet you."

Hannah explained that Miss White was living in the attic room and read aloud in the dining room most evenings. "She has some wonderful books!" she exclaimed.

"I would love to see them, if I may," said Thomas.

"You may borrow whatever you wish," said Miss White graciously. "Perhaps you can join us after supper and tell us about Boston. I have never been there."

Thomas regarded Miss White evenly, a smile upon his lips, but he was wary. He noticed her distinct British accent. Could he trust this woman? Could she be a spy among them, living right here at Hart's Tavern, and listening to every word they said?

Nodding his head slightly he said, "Indeed! Well, then, I shall have to educate the teacher!" He would warn his father to keep an eye on her.

Then they laughed together. Hannah felt at that moment that she was so happy that she wanted to capture the feeling forever. She looked at the fireplace and felt that its warmth matched the glow in her heart. If only things could stay this way.

# Chapter Twenty-four

The very next day Hannah stopped at the post office where Miss Fisk handed her a letter. It was from Adeline! Hannah could not wait until she was home to read it. She had heard nothing from Adeline since her family had left New Kensington for Middletown, Connecticut. Mr. Squires came back to town from time to time, but otherwise their large home was closed up, the lovely furniture and paintings covered with sheets.

Hannah sat on a bench in the dry goods store and opened the letter. Adeline had written it several weeks before. Hannah recognized Adeline's delicate script handwriting on the fine parchment paper. She read,

*October 31, 1775*

*Dear Hannah,*

*It has taken me quite a while to write to you because of the many adjustments I have had to make here in Connecticut. Now that I have my writing materials, which I purchased in the small village a few miles away, I have decided to set pen to paper.*

*The Atkinson family has been kind, especially Ophelia, who is about my age. My mother and Mrs. Atkinson get on well. Nevertheless it is crowded in this house, with four adults, seven children, and assorted slaves and servants. I share a small room with Margaret. There is room in the wardrobe for only two of my frocks, so the others must remain in the large chest. I keep busy with my embroidery, but it does not hold my interest. I occasionally walk the grounds, although*

*I still have not been able to regain my strength since my illness last fall. The weather has been foul lately, so I have not been out, lest I catch a chill.*

*I have the most exciting news, dear Hannah! I have started classes with the Atkinson children, in the drawing room downstairs. The teacher is a recent graduate of Yale College named Nathan Hale. He is a young man to whom one cannot help be attracted, with fine, flaxen hair and eyes the color of indigo. Mr. Hale is from a prosperous farm in Coventry. He has eight brothers and sisters, so he is not intimidated by the number of students he must teach at once. Aside from the Atkinson children and myself there are six others from the area who join us each morning for three hours, a total of thirteen students. Mr. Hale is a wonderful teacher. He is a devout Patriot who becomes rather ardent in his discussions of freedom and the events that are taking place between here and Boston. I wonder if he is acquainted with your brother, Thomas. I must ask him. I am quite sure they resided in Boston at the same time, at least for a while.*

*Dear Hannah. I miss your visits. I also miss my pianoforte, for there is none here. I keep busy trying to amuse the children and helping Mother and Mrs. Atkinson as much as I can. I am not interested in spinning and embroidery, however, so it is a struggle sometimes to sit with them for long hours and attempt these endeavors. Soon I hope Father will bring me some watercolors because I envision spending time in my sunny room, painting pleasant scenes. In spring, when the weather is mild, I hope to paint en plein air -- in the outdoors. I have tried to keep up with my French. Mr. Hale works with me on that, too.*

*I do hope you and your family are well. Please write to me.*

*Your devoted friend,*
*Adeline Justine Squires*

Hannah folded the long letter carefully. She saw that Miss Fisk was watching her like a cat. Hannah wondered what her face revealed as she had read the letter – perhaps an expression of relief for Adeline's well being as well as interest in what she had to say, but also, she had to admit, a touch of envy. Adeline was living at the home of a wealthy family, surrounded by children, and apparently safe from the Redcoats and Hessians who appeared more and more frequently in New Kensington. Adeline's only inconvenience, thought Hannah wryly, was that she did not have her pianoforte. And what of Adeline's interest in Mr. Nathan Hale? Was he taking the place of Miss White as well as Hannah in Adeline's affections? Adeline had shown little interest in the Sons of Liberty and all the news of Boston until now. She had said she thought it was a great bore. But now it seemed Mr. Hale had changed all that. And only last night Thomas had said he was going to Connecticut to meet Nathan Hale, too. Would he also meet Adeline? Hannah felt ashamed of her jealousy.

Hannah knew she could go to Connecticut if she wished, especially after the discussion last night. Her father had asked her if she wanted to go there right after Adeline and her family had left. He knew a family near Middletown that would take her in, not too far from the William Floyd family, the Atkinsons, and Adeline Squires and her mother. But Hannah had said no. Despite what Adeline said in her letter, Hannah knew she would not be happy there. Her place was at Hart's Tavern, with her father. He needed her and she needed him. Perhaps in the future she would think differently. She did, indeed, want a life of adventure one day. But Hannah suspected that she would not need to go far to find it, not with the rumblings of war that were getting closer.

Hannah realized that she was staring out the window, gripping Adeline's letter tightly in her hands. Miss Fisk cleared her throat. "Everything all right?" she asked, tilting her head ever so slightly. Hannah almost expected to hear her purr in anticipation of what she might say in reply.

"Everything is fine, thank you Miss Fisk." Hannah knew of course that she had read the return address. "I will be writing back to Adeline Squires very soon."

But Hannah never wrote back. Only three days later she learned that Adeline had died.

# Chapter Twenty-five

"Papa, what happened?" asked Hannah, her eyes wide with disbelief. Her heart was beating rapidly, as if she had just run all the way across the meadow. She couldn't take it all in. It was as if she were in a terrible dream where everything is all wrong. Surely, what her father was saying could not be real.

"Dr. Myers said Adeline came down with fever again, similar to the one that took hold of her several weeks ago," he explained quietly. "The doctor in Connecticut undertook an even more aggressive series of bleedings, to rid Adeline of the bad humours that possessed her. But it did no good."

Hannah stood rigid in disbelief. A horrible thought entered her mind – what if the doctors were wrong? What if bleeding didn't help, but only made things worse? She could not hold back the blasphemous thoughts that raced through her mind. She was thinking that if Goody Garlicke had been able to care for Adeline then she would be well. Goody Garlicke, the old woman whom some people said was a witch, had been known to cure ills when doctors could not. Hannah shuddered at the image of Adeline stretched out, leeches on her pale arms, her face ghastly white and translucent. Hannah hoped she had not suffered. She could not hold back the sobs that shook through her thin body.

Peter Hart was grieved to see her this way. This girl, his daughter, had lost her mother to fever, and now she had lost her best friend. He felt a swell of anger rise in his chest and silently cursed fate. Sometimes he did not understand God's will and motivation. Sometimes he did not understand the church's teachings at all.

"Come, Hannah. Let us go inside. There is nothing we can do." He led her into the dining room where she sat alone at the big table. In a while Mrs. Hewitt appeared with a pot of herbal tea, and sat beside her. Then Miss White appeared in the doorway, her face ashen. She crossed the room swiftly and took Hannah into her arms, and the two of them wept. Mrs. Hewitt put the corner of her handkerchief to her eye. Then the three of them sat at the table in silence as Mrs. Hewitt poured the herbal tea into their cups. For once there was no talk of chores. For once there was no hurrying or bustling about to get dinner or go to work in the barn. They sat there until the sun went down. Eventually Mrs. Hewitt brought bowls of soup from the pot hanging over the fire. Hannah recited her prayers that night, but behind her words was the silent question, "Why?"

Two nights later, eight people were seated at the long oak table in Hart's Tavern. It was a bitter cold Saturday afternoon in late November. For the first time that fall a fire roared in both fireplaces. Evie sat on her stool at the hearth on the west side of the room, knitting, and within earshot of the conversation, ready to fetch whatever might be required from the kitchen. Thomas sat at the head of the table. Next to him on his right was Peter Hart, and on his left, Hannah. Next sat Mr. And Mrs. Hewitt. Beside them sat Jeremy Moore, hoping to get news for his broadsheets, and Dr. Myers, who wanted to hear about the smallpox epidemic that was sweeping through Yale College. He wondered if that was the disease that had taken Adeline's life. Miss White sat beside Dr. Myers. She wanted to know about the situation in Boston, and how it would affect her students' schooling here in New Kensington.

The group was gathered to welcome Thomas home, and to hear what he had to say about his experiences in Boston. As far as Thomas knew, all of them were trustworthy Patriots.

"It is good to be back," he said. "Classes at Harvard are sporadic now, since King George has appointed Thomas Gage governor, and the damnable Intolerable Acts have been imposed upon the colonies."

"What does this mean?" asked Miss White. "What has been imposed?"

"Many things," said Thomas. "As all of you know, the port of Boston has been ordered closed. The people are forbidden to have Town Meetings, except for once a year. The King has decided that all capital crimes will be tried in England, not in the colony where the crime has been committed. Colonial courts will have almost no authority. The royal governor will now appoint our local officials, instead of them being elected. And the Quartering Act has been extended. This means that instead of eventually leaving, British troops will now remain here permanently. This act affects all of us, since British troops are at this very moment taking over just about all of New Kensington."

Thomas waited a while for all of this to sink in. When the murmurings had died down, he continued. "Whilst in Boston I met a man, the town silversmith and owner of a copper mine. He has a thriving business and a large family. And he can ride! He is one of the messengers of the Committees of Correspondence." Thomas' voice trailed off, as if he had decided against revealing more.

"What is this man's name?" asked Dr. Myers.

Thomas said nothing, but reached into his pocket and brought out a leather pouch, which he set upon the table. He reached into the pouch and brought out a large spoon, highly polished and with a stem and bowl so finely wrought of shining silver that it made the pewter utensils at the table look dull and clumsy. He handed the spoon to his father. "There is a bowl that goes with it," he said. "It is my gift to you, Father, and Hannah." Peter Hart handed the spoon to Hannah, who turned it over and over in her hands. It was almost as large as a ladle. It had no ornate decoration. Instead, its lines were clean and fine. On the back of the handle was engraved, "Paul Revere."

"Mr. Revere lives on the north side of town," Thomas went on. "He carried the news of the Boston Tea Party south to New York and Philadelphia, after getting no sleep the night before. He was one of the so-called Indians who dumped tea into the harbor."

"Tell us about the "Tea Party," said Miss White. "I've heard about it, but surely you must know more of the details."

Thomas raised his eyebrows as if surprised by the question. But he went on, "As you know, the colonists despised the Tea Act. Not only would we have to pay a tax on tea, the Tea Act would have given a monopoly to the governor's close friends and relatives who would control the sale of all tea. What would be next? We knew the Tea Act was a ruse and we wanted no part of it. No one wanted the tea ships to land in Boston. The tea party began at the Old South Meeting House. The participants and others went to Griffin's Wharf, where three tea ships were docked."

"What were the names of the ships?" asked Hannah.

"The Dartmouth, the Eleanor and the Beaver," replied Thomas, perhaps a bit too quickly, Hannah thought. Had her brother been part of this event? Hannah suspected that Thomas was in more danger than he let on.

Thomas continued, "About 120 men and boys, dressed as Mohawks with lighted torches boarded the ships. They were well organized. This sabotage was well planned. They boarded the ships and warned the officer on duty to get out of the way. Then some of the men and boys broke open the tea chests while others waded into the harbor, making sure that the tea sank below the surface. One man was caught stuffing his pockets with tea, and he was thrown into the harbor as well. Thousands of people watched what was happening from the shore. When it was all over, there was quiet, not loud rejoicing, as some would think. The Patriots knew the British would retaliate for the deed."

"How much tea was dumped?" asked Mrs. Hewitt, her eyes wide. Nothing interested her more than food and drink. She was thinking of all that wasted tea.

"More than 46 tons of tea leaves, I understand," said Thomas. "Someone calculated that it would be the equivalent of more than

18 and a half million cups of tea, valued at almost ten thousand British pounds sterling."

Mrs. Hewitt started fanning herself with her handkerchief, as if she were about to faint at the loss of so much tea. She said, "And to think that I've not had a good cup of tea since then!" she exclaimed.

Hannah almost smiled at how Mrs. Hewitt seemed to feel the colonists engaged in the Boston Tea Party just to inconvenience her, but she did not. Hannah knew this event was something too important and too significant, to smile about.

Now it was Peter Hart's turn to speak. Until now he had said nothing. "What else have you learned, son?" he asked.

"I have been to several meetings at Faneuil Hall," replied Thomas. "Sam Adams, one of the great Patriots, often speaks there. The funeral for the victims of the Boston Massacre was held there. Now it is where the Committee of Correspondence assembles."

"Including members from New Kensington?" asked Jeremy Moore.

"Yes," replied Thomas. "But news and information must pass through New York City on its way here, and it may be out of date by the time it gets here."

"I want to publish more news of the colonies," said Jeremy. "I'd like to double the size of our weekly broadsheets."

Thomas nodded. "That would be excellent," he said. "It is important for the citizens to be informed about what is going on beyond their towns."
He paused for a moment, and then sighed and said quietly, "I predict that in the future communication will be more and more important, and delivered in ways faster than we can even imagine. But right now I suspect that even the small town of New Kensington will feel the effects of what has happened in Boston."

"Are you going back?" asked Mr. Hewitt. He was so quiet that Hannah forgot he was there. His wig was slightly askew, his watery blue eyes half closed. He seemed wistful, thought Hannah, as if he wished he could go with Thomas.

"Yes, I'll go back. I want to continue my classes. I want to study law and perhaps enter politics. I have many friends now in Boston."

"But your family is here," said Peter.

Thomas hesitated. "Yes. That is why I returned. But there is something else . . ." His voice trailed off. "Perhaps this conversation should continue another time."

Mrs. Hewitt took that as a hint and pushed back her chair, and headed for the kitchen. Evie took her cue and joined her. Soon a good, hot supper would be served. Then Dr. Myers and Jeremy Moore would head back to town together. The sky outside was already dark and moonless. The room grew quiet, except for the crackle of the fire. Hannah felt thrilled to have been a part of this conversation. It meant that she was no longer a child in the eyes of her father and brother. But she also felt the grim tug of fear. What were the Patriots getting themselves into? The Boston Tea Party and all of its aftermath were nothing to laugh at or feel smug about. Hannah knew King George was powerful, and the colonists had defied him. Once again, she felt a longing to return to the past, to a time when she was small, and safe, when her only problem was a skinned knee or a spilled glass of milk, and her mother was there to stroke her hair and tell her everything would be all right, But Hannah knew that one could never go back, not in time or place. It was a harsh lesson that she would have to learn many times.

# Chapter Twenty-Six

Christmas was coming. The dining room of Hart's Tavern was filled with the pleasant, resinous scent of pine from the boughs Peter Hart had cut and placed in the windows. The mantle and woodwork were polished with beeswax. The floors had been swept. Evie and Mrs. Hewitt were busy baking mince pies and hasty pudding. Several hams had been salted and stored for the winter, but one was boiling now for dinner. The delicious smells and festive air gave Hannah a sense of excitement as she helped to prepare food for the evening's guests.

The Christmas season lasted from Christmas Eve until January 6, Epiphany. During these days the colonists went to church almost every day. There would be feasts and singing, except, of course in the Quaker Meeting House. The Quakers did not believe in singing inside their gathering place. Besides, it was filled with Redcoats who had set up lodging there.

Mrs. Penelope Hyde, wife of the wealthy Salem merchant Henry Hyde who had made his fortune trading cod and lumber for molasses and sugar cane in the West Indies, had organized a festive Christmas market the last two years. Some said the market was sinful, with its colorful decorations, mulled wine, and music provided by local fiddlers, but Mrs. Hyde dismissed those comments with a wave of her hand. Now, even the cranky postmistress, Miss Fisk, joined in the festivities, putting pine branches in the windows of her shop, and stocking special honey cakes for the children. Today, Hannah would go into town with Miss White and Mrs. Hewitt. She had six pence in the little drawstring purse she kept in her pocket. She would use the money to buy small gifts for everyone, to be opened on Christmas morning.

The day was bright and cloudless, the light of the low winter sun sparkling on the snow-covered meadow that led to Melancholy Hollow. Hannah sat in the sledge between Miss White and the plump Mrs. Hewitt, who adjusted the blanket that covered their legs. When all were seated comfortably, Mr. Hewitt cracked the whip and the horses lurched down the rutted road to New Kensington.

Honeycomb and Badger huffed and snorted as they pulled the sledge, making new tracks in the untouched snow, their breath coming out of their nostrils in steamy clouds. Great pines, their boughs heavy with snow, lined the road. As the sledge passed under them, a scattering of sparkling snow dust fell on Hannah's eyelashes and on Miss White's hair. Years later, Hannah recalled this ride, and how on this sunny day she had experienced what could only be called pure happiness. The feeling was almost something she could taste, like honey warmed by the sun.

She found herself humming and tapping her feet to her own song. Soon Miss White joined in and the two were singing a jolly tune. Even Mrs. Hewitt wore a smile. The sledge veered and turned, the sound of its rails making a soft shushing sound, picking up speed as it went down small hills. The trees rushed by. Hannah felt invigorated by it all and didn't want the ride to end.

At last the sledge skidded to a stop, directly in front of the print shop, where there was a place to tether the horses. Hannah and Miss White hopped down while Mrs. Hewitt followed more slowly.

"Morning!" Jeremy's voice sang out of the shop's window. "How are you ladies this fine day?"

"Very well, thank you," replied Miss White. Hannah said nothing, but smiled and waved.

"Stop back later?" Jeremy sounded hopeful. "Have a cup of coffee with me and Mr. McDowell."

"Thank you, yes!" said Miss White. Mrs. Hewitt beamed, for she assumed that she was invited too. She hoped there might be a drop of wine along with the coffee.

The trio made their way toward the Town Square, while Mr. Hewitt headed back to Hart's Tavern. He would meet them later. The three women walked to the tree where the latest broadsheets were posted. These were more recent than the ones hanging on the wall of the inn. They stopped to take a look. One was written by a member of the Continental Congress. Violet read aloud,

*The scandalous and wicked practice of seizing the property of the good inhabitants of the colony, already too much distressed, under the pretense of military prize render it necessary that some rule must be established. One fourth the value of any horse, ox, cow, heifer, sheep, hog or lamb . . .*

"What is that all about, Miss White?" asked Hannah.

"It is about the unlawful seizure of farm animals by Redcoats or Hessians. There is not much that can be done about it, but the Continental Congress is trying to provide some compensation to the farmers."

Hannah nodded, thinking how terrible she would feel if someone took away Badger and Honeycomb, or even one of the goats or sheep.

Hannah and her teacher walked arm in arm into the street, towards the shops. They stopped in front of Adeline's house, now completely taken over by the Redcoats. Hannah felt as if a dark shadow had passed over her, but she was determined not to become morose on this beautiful day. Adeline would not have wanted that. Instead, Hannah pictured Adeline, in her yellow dress, playing her favorite piece on the pianoforte. She smiled at the thought. Turning to Miss White she said," I was just thinking of Adeline, and how pretty she was," she said.

Suddenly a snowball flew past Hannah, nearly striking her on the side of her head. She turned around angrily, and saw some boys near the big tree in the center of the square. They ran away when Hannah bent to make a snowball of her own. She took aim and let go, hitting one of the boys on the seat of his pants. Hannah and Miss White laughed and continued on their way.

"Those boys should be in school," said Miss White. "They stopped coming to lessons in Mrs. Braithwaite's parlor when the Redcoats took over, and now that I hold classes in the inn I have not seen them at all, especially that naughty Jack Jewell. He is a bright boy. His brother, George, is just lazy. They haven't been the same since their father died."

"Are they the sons of Polly Jewell, the woman I met at church?"

"Yes," replied Miss White. "Polly's husband Sam was stricken down last May. A wound he suffered festered and caused a fever that eventually caused his heart to stop. Polly blames it on the Redcoat who knocked him from his horse in a skirmish in Brooklyn. Her husband was a Patriot, one of the Sons of Liberty. Polly moved here where she had some relatives. She has vowed to carry on his cause with the Daughters of Liberty. I went to one of their meetings."

"Have you seen Mrs. Braithwaite and Bea?" asked Hannah.

"No," said Miss White. "That is one of the things I wish to do soon. Bea is deaf, not feeble minded. There is much she can learn and do. I have written to my father, asking him if there is anything that can help her. There are some new hearing aids for deaf people."

The two young women continued on their way down the street. Unbeknownst to them, they were being watched by many who thought what a pretty pair they were. Two Redcoats, in particular, had their eyes on them.

Hannah and Miss White continued on their way to the dry goods shop. There were very few new items, since trade had slowed down since the soldiers had come to town. But Hannah saw a bolt of bright blue cotton. She wished she had the time and money to sew herself a new dress.

Miss Fisk stood behind her counter, her plain face pale in the light. "There is a letter for you, Miss White," she said. Violet turned and eagerly took the letter. "It is from father!" she said. She slid a finger under the flap, breaking the wax seal. She read the letter while Hannah and Miss Fisk waited eagerly. Mrs. Hewitt had pricked up her ears, too, and craned her neck to see the letter. Any news was devoured, but a letter from England! This was rare, indeed. Violet White looked up from her letter, her eyes shining. "My baby sister is well," she said. That was all she said. She tucked the letter into her bag, to Miss Fisk's disappointment.

Hannah continued looking all around the store. She chose some sugar pigs for Evie and Mrs. Hewitt. What to buy for Thomas and her father? That was difficult. She studied a display of belt and shoe buckles, imagining the quality of ones wrought by Paul Revere compared to these rough ones. No, these would not do.

As Hannah continued looking at the goods, Miss White went back to the counter where Miss Fisk stood with the bolts of fabric. The teacher said something quietly to Miss Fisk, and then opened her purse. Miss Fisk beamed a rare smile and nodded her head.

Hannah turned and noticed the smile, wondering what Miss White had said to the woman to make her so happy. It seemed that everyone loved Miss White!

They spent the rest of the afternoon pleasantly, ending with strong cups of coffee and crackers with Jeremy and Hiram McDowell at the print shop. The setting was less than pristine, but the coffee and company were fine. Everyone laughed and laughed at Mr. McDowell's jokes and scandalous imitations of King George. Hannah was sorry to see the day draw to a close, but soon it was time to get back to the inn and help serve dinner to the guests. Evie would be waiting for them.

As Mr. Hewitt pulled up in the sledge Hannah was still happy, because she had Christmas to look forward to.

# Chapter Twenty-Seven

The wind that blows and shifts through the grass on the dunes around the Great Bay makes a sound like a sigh. Sometimes it whirls into small cyclones, picking up leaves that twirl in a dance that Wyanjoy knew had magical properties. When the spring moon was full, the girls and women of her tribe imitated this dance near a fire, while the men sat nearby singing and tapping their drums in a rhythm that became hypnotic.

According to legend, girls and women long ago danced through the night, faster and faster, until they spun themselves into birch trees. There were several versions of the tale, but Wyanjoy's favorite was that the women were dancing to avoid entrapment by men of another tribe who wished to carry them off. As long as they danced, they were safe, and could wait until husbands of their own choice appeared to them.

Birch trees were scarce in Melancholy Hollow, but a group of nine of them grew in a spot in the woods where the ground was high. Their slender trunks and delicate leaves that fluttered in the smallest breeze left Wyanjoy with no doubt that these trees were indeed enchanted.

On this day, in late December, the sky was deep gray, like the stones of the outcroppings by the Great Bay. The air was dense with moisture, with a chill that seeped through Wyanjoy's deerskin coat. Soon snow would fall and settle thickly on the leafless branches of the birches. Some of them would break.

Nearly everyone in Wyanjoy's village was sick. Some of the able-bodied men had deserted the tribe to become guides for the white farmers who were also soldiers. They had traveled north, past Manhattan Island, to trade furs and seek healthier lands. Some had become soldiers, fighting alongside the Redcoats, while others joined the colonists. The numbers of her tribe were growing small.

Wyanjoy knew it was inevitable that she, too, would become ill with the mysterious sickness that had plagued her people, as would her child, who would be born soon. She had felt the first pangs of labor in the early afternoon. She was surprised at this because she had calculated there would be one more moon before the baby would appear. She did not worry, though, because she knew that many women have false pains and must wait out their time. Then she looked toward the longhouse at the end of road. This was the house of sickness. Wyanjoy had not set foot in there, not even to see her sister who had shown signs of the pox two weeks ago. She stayed, instead, in a hut at the edge of the tribe. But it was a cold place, with only a small fire, and Wyanjoy knew her baby would not survive there. This evil sickness was taking over their once thriving village.

Another, stronger contraction swept through her body, starting at her back and tightening her belly into a fist. Now Wyanjoy realized that this labor was not false. Her time was near. Her baby would not wait for another moon to pass. He would be born this night. She made a decision. She took the small leather pouch containing her pearls from its hiding place and hung it around her neck. Then, wrapping herself in as many furs as she could, and covering her head with a wool shawl, she ventured out into the snow. She took a walking stick to guide her, and her old dog, who followed her through the reeds of Melancholy Hollow toward the meadow where Goody Garlicke lived. Wyanjoy believed that if she could get to the old woman's cottage her baby would be born in safety. But why had she waited so long? She prayed to the spirits to guide her through the storm to the home of Goody Garlicke.

She walked slowly into the wind, grasping the stick, leaning upon it. Her large belly felt heavier, because the weight had shifted; her back hurt. The snow began to stick to her boots. She was already growing cold, and she had to walk up the long, slow rise over the meadow to Goody's cottage. Each time a contraction bore down upon her she stopped and breathed deeply. Then, as she was taught to do during times of hardship, Wyanjoy took her mind to a different place. She tried to imagine the warm summer days when the turtles and sunfish swam in the shallows of the river near the marsh of Melancholy Hollow, how they would show off their brilliant red, blue, and yellow flecks in the bright summer sun. Even the big torps – the giant, meaty turtles that her people roasted on spits over fires – could not escape observation in the sunlit water. The shiny pebbles seemed to make the clear water sing where the river began. Later, downstream in the marsh, the water turned into black ooze where Wyanjoy dug in her toes to poke up fat eels. She thought about the raccoons, muskrats, and red fox that lived there. She remembered the beautiful swans, osprey, red tailed hawks, and white herons. She recalled the green-necked wood ducks, the red winged blackbirds, and little kingfishers. All these creatures were part of her summer world. Where were they now?

The snow began to swirl faster and faster as the wind picked up. The pains were coming faster and stronger, too. Wyanjoy felt her knees buckling beneath her. She knew then that she would not make it to Goody Garlicke's house. She would give birth to her child, here in the snow, and here, together, they would die.

Wyanjoy was becoming disoriented. Which way was south? She searched the sky for a clue, but the thick snow blinded her. Only her feet told her the land was getting steeper, the meadow closer. She turned around and saw a shadow that she recognized – a big oak tree that had blown down in another storm. It was the only possible shelter nearby. Crying out to her dog, she made her way to the tree.

# Chapter Twenty-eight

Snow swirled around Hart's Tavern, blanketing the roof and drifting against the fir trees. Icy gusts of wind rattled the windowpanes and blew the flakes into small cyclones. Inside, Evie hauled more logs to the fire. The inn was full tonight. A stagecoach from Boston had arrived, fortunately before the storm. Several people had to double up in the rooms upstairs, and Hannah had to give up her space and move behind the kitchen with Evie, something she rarely did.

Hannah sat by the fire with Miss White, who had taken up knitting. She was making a blanket for her baby sister Nicole. Hannah had her embroidery in her lap. She had made little progress on the piece she was working on, attentive instead to the guests who were talking and laughing as they sat around the tables, awaiting their dinner. Some of them played cards or dice, and smoked one of the long clay pipes from the rack beside the door. The ale flowed generously. Hannah felt warm and content to be there, as the blizzard raged outside.

Suddenly, the door blew open with a bang. Hannah couldn't believe her eyes. Standing there in her black garments covered with snow was Goody Garlicke, the recluse! As far as Hannah knew, she had never been to the inn, and rarely ventured from her cottage in Melancholy Hollow. Hannah got up and slammed the door behind Goody. She tried to lead the old woman to a chair, but Goody Garlicke would not sit down.

Between gasps for breath she cried, "There's an Indian woman who just gave birth in the snow! She's a quarter mile down the marsh! My dogs found her."

Without a word Peter Hart pulled his coat, hat and scarf from the pegs by the door. "Get the wagon," he said to Phineas Hewitt. I'll be right there!"

"I am coming, too, Father!" said Hannah. "Evie! Get blankets from the beds. "Prepare a room. Boil water. Find dry clothes. Hurry!"

Evie scurried into their room behind the kitchen. Miss White quickly put down her knitting and climbed the steps to her attic room to get a blanket from her own trunk. Hannah wrapped herself in shawls and two woolen cloaks and joined her father outside where Hewitt had pulled up the wagon hitched to Badger and Honeycomb. The horses were not accustomed to the harness in such weather, and stamped their hooves nervously.

Hannah wondered how long the Indian had been out in the snow. How could a newborn infant and its mother survive in the freezing cold? Hannah knew little of the native people around New Kensington. There were so few of them left. The situation was so unreal it felt like a dream.

Hannah lifted her skirts and climbed into the wagon, which was covered with a tarpaulin. She huddled under her shawls with Goody Garlicke as her father drove the wagon over the snow covered, rutted road. Peter Hart urged on the two horses who neighed and reared as they strained against their harness to pull the wagon along the rough path. They bumped over a tree root with a bounce that nearly sent Hannah flying out of the wagon.

Finally Goody shouted, "Here! Turn here!"

The horses pulled to the left and the wagon began to slide sideways. Afraid it would topple over into the deep snow, Peter pulled the horses to a stop. "Hannah, wait here! I'll have to walk the rest of the way."

"No, Father, I am coming." Hannah climbed out of the wagon, as her father lifted the old woman out.

Goody pointed southeast. "She's down there, where there's a fallen tree."

There was no moon, and the pale light from Peter's lantern illuminated only a few feet ahead as the three figures trudged through the snow. Hannah hardly felt her feet. She clutched the blankets. She was so cold that she could not imagine anyone surviving, especially a tiny baby.

After what seemed like hours they could hear dogs barking in the distance. "We're almost there," croaked Goody, pointing to the edge of the meadow.

At last they came to the place where the fallen oak lay. Peter ran ahead, with Hannah following along. Goody had stopped in her tracks to catch her breath. Hannah watched as her father's light bobbed in the snowy air, down into the hollow of the fallen tree. She pulled up her skirts, heavy with snow, and tried to run the rest of the way. At last she was at the base of the uprooted tree. What she saw made her gasp. There, wrapped in animal skins and huddled between two dogs, lay an Indian woman, with her newborn baby. Without a word Peter Hart handed the lantern to Hannah and lifted the woman and her baby into his arms. Wyanjoy closed her eyes and let her head drop against his shoulder. She clutched her baby to her chest as Hannah draped a blanket over him. With the two dogs barking at their heels, the strange procession made their way back to the wagon.

Hannah and Goody bundled Wyanjoy between them in the wagon as it bumped its way back to the inn. The ride seemed endless. The baby was quiet. Hannah wondered it if was alive. How long had the Indian lain in the snow? Why was she out in the marsh, alone? Hannah realized that she had always taken the native people for granted. They came and went into town in their odd clothes, speaking their strange language. Some of them worked as servants. Now, some of the men and boys had become guides for the Patriots. Others had sided with the Tories. Hannah had never looked upon them as people like herself. She had heard their numbers were dwindling, but she honestly could not say that she cared. Yet here, tonight, in the middle of December, lay a woman and child in her father's wagon. She was responsible for them. Why had God put them in her path? Hannah shifted her position and put her hand on the woman's forehead. It was neither cold nor warm. She supposed that was a good thing.

Then another problem occurred to her. Where could they stay at the inn? All the rooms were filled, even overfilled. She remembered how they had made room for Miss White in the attic when the Redcoats had moved into Mrs. Braithwaite's boarding house. Now there was only one place left -- the barn. It was warm in there, with the two horses, four goats, two sheep and a lamb. Hannah would tell Evie to fetch coals to put in a bucket for heat. With dry bedding the Indian and her baby could be made comfortable.

At last the silhouette of Hart's Tavern came into view, its welcoming windows glowing amber from the warm firelight within. Peter Hart pulled the horses to a stop outside the barn, slid open its heavy door, and led the snorting horses inside, where Hewitt would rub them down. Hannah ran to get Evie with the hot coals and blankets.

The small bucket of coals did not provide as much warmth as the heat from the bodies of the animals. The sheep and goats lay close to Wyanjoy and her baby, a boy, along with the two dogs, who were not interested in the sheep, but in the two beef bones Hannah had brought to them from the kitchen. Evie and Miss White had brought all the spare quilts they could find, as well as a jug of hot broth and hunks of fresh bread and goat cheese. Wyanjoy was hungry after her ordeal, which was a good sign, thought Hannah.

Goody Garlicke could not return to her cottage in the storm, so she, too, would remain in the barn. She could look after Wyanjoy during the night. So Hannah left them there, a strange vignette in the glow of the lamplight. A mother and infant lying on blankets in the straw, surrounded by animals, with an old woman in dark garments sitting by her side. Hannah smiled to herself. A rush of happiness swept though her at the sight of the new life, safe in their barn. May God bless them all, she thought.

# Chapter Twenty-nine

Christmas had come and gone, but Wyanjoy and her baby stayed in the barn for a while longer. Hannah visited them every day. Although they did not speak the same language, the two young women bonded quickly. On the third day, Wyanjoy handed her baby to Hannah. "His name is Peter," she said haltingly. She had named her son after Hannah's father.

Hannah held the tiny boy in her arms, and ran her forefinger along the side of his face. Suddenly he thrust his arms into the air, opened his eyes, and yawned. Then he snuggled back down into Hannah's arms and sighed. Hannah, Wyanjoy and Goody smiled at his expression of pure contentment.

Wyanjoy was also growing stronger. One day when the weather was clear and sunny, mother and son were ready to leave. Peter Hart bundled them into the sledge to take them over the snow-covered meadow to Goody Garlicke's little cottage. There they would remain in safety, at least until spring.

That afternoon Peter Hart and some men loaded a pile of heavy sacks into the corner of the barn, and hid them under a pile of hay. Hannah did not see them, however. She was busy in the kitchen with Evie and Mrs. Hewitt.

One Sunday during the first week of January, Hannah came upon her father and Thomas in the barn. They were lifting the heavy, bulky sacks from under the hay and onto the wagon.

"What are you doing?" asked Hannah. It was most unusual for her father to be working in this manner, especially on a Sunday morning.

"We are going to church," came his terse reply. Hannah raised her eyebrows in surprise. Peter Hart seldom went to church.

"To church? With a wagonload of . . ." Hannah's voice trailed off. Suddenly the realization occurred to her that her father and Thomas were planning to do more than attend the church service. They were no doubt delivering something.

"What is in the sacks?" she asked.

"Nothing you need concern yourself with."

"Please, tell me!" demanded Hannah, who was growing alarmed.

Her father set down the last sack and turned to face her. Thomas leaned against the wagon. "All right, then, he said. We are delivering arms and ammunition to be hidden in the basement of the church. I did not want to tell you because this must remain a secret. But had I not told you now, undoubtedly your curiosity would have gotten the better of you and you might've gone around town talking about it."

Hannah felt herself growing red. "Father, I am not a child! Do I not help you with the petticoat signal? I have a right to know what is going on. Remember what Miss White read to us last night after dinner. I want to help the Patriots!"

"Then get your cloak and come with us. Having you along will be good cover. Miss White is coming as well, to meet her friend, Polly Jewell. All will be revealed to you in good time."

Hannah ran into the house to put on more clothing, her heart thumping. She was going to be a part of the Patriot cause!

The night before, as they sat together in the corner of the dining room where it was now their custom to read with Miss White and discuss recent events, Thomas had pulled a small pamphlet from his shirt pocket and said, "This, my friends, is the book that is being read in all of the colonies. This book articulates why we must break from Mother England. It was written by Thomas Paine, and published most recently."

The book had only 47 pages. On the back was printed, *The Free and Independent States of America*. It was the first time Hannah had seen such words in print. It was the first time she had grasped the concept that the little town of New Kensington, which had always been ruled by the magistrates of a King named George in faraway England, could change. One day people would vote for their own laws.

Hannah and the others listened, almost awestruck, as her brother read from the thin volume. "Why should colonial Englishmen not have the same rights as English who live in England? Why cannot colonial Englishmen retain their right to trial by jury? Why should we be subjected to general search warrants? Why are we taxed and taxed, yet have no say in electing our own representatives? The fact that we immigrated to the New World should not preclude our rights as English citizens!"

The inn was full that night, so Thomas had a large audience. "Hear! Hear!" said the listeners, as he read and elucidated the words of Thomas Paine. His words were like the wind on glowing embers. That night those words convinced many who had been undecided about breaking free from England to declare themselves to be Patriots.

When she returned to the wagon, wrapped in her warmest cloak, her father and Thomas were waiting. The sacks of weapons were hidden under a tarpaulin. Hannah did not ask where they had come from, but suspected that some of the late night guests who met with her father had brought them, maybe even had stolen them from the British. Perhaps Evie's friend, the runaway slave, was one. At the thought of Evie, Hannah turned toward the house, and saw her standing in the doorway. She gave a little wave, and Evie waved back. As the wagon bumped along the road, Hannah wondered again where this would all lead.

At last the wagon stopped in front of the church and Hannah got out. Her father and Thomas snapped the reins and continued down the road until they could turn and go to the rear of the building. Hannah did not go inside the church. She walked nonchalantly down the road until she, too, turned the corner to go to the rear of the building. There was the wagon, next to the trap door that led to the cellar of the church. Miss White was there with a small, white-haired woman whom Hannah recognized as

Polly Jewell. The two women lifted the trap door while the two men unloaded their cargo. They quickly closed the door leading to the cellar once Thomas and her father had descended the steps. Then, much to Hannah's surprise, Polly Jewell jumped up on the wagon and snapped the reins. She drove the wagon down the road, towards the stable, where the horses would remain until the church service was over. She nodded at Hannah as she passed. Hannah was surprised how young her face was, considering she had white hair. She was not only strong, but beautiful!

Miss White came up beside Hannah. "Let's go into the church, shall we?" she said, taking Hannah by the arm. The young teacher and her student made a pretty pair as they walked arm and arm into the church. Soon they were joined in their pew by Peter and Thomas Hart, and then by Polly Jewell. Many eyes of the congregation were upon them. They were an attractive bunch. Two soldiers in red coats, who often attended services here, where the sermons were usually pro-British, especially noticed the women. Hannah felt her heart beating fast from the knowledge of what they had done. She took several deep breaths in an effort to calm herself. "We are safe," she told herself. "After all, we are in the Episcopal Church – the Church of England."

# Chapter Thirty

Three days passed uneventfully. On the fourth day, the air was still, with a heaviness that signaled a storm was brewing. Hannah remembered later that everything had seemed normal. She was in the kitchen; Evie was near the well. Peter Hart and Thomas were working nearby at the edge of the meadow.

The peace was broken by a sudden pounding on the door. Two Redcoats and two Hessians pushed it open and burst into the room. "We are taking over this inn for our troops," said the black haired Redcoat. "Step aside." At first Hannah said nothing, and stood frozen. She regarded the four men in front of her. This was the day they had dreaded, but the day she knew was inevitable.

She reached for the shotgun that her father kept beside the fireplace. "You'll not enter, Sir," she said, standing her ground and pointing the rifle at the soldiers.

The big Hessian laughed and twisted the weapon right out of her hands. The men walked into the dining room. They seemed to take up all the space with their boots and big coats, and their guns that they waved around as they spoke. They laughed loudly, too, and soon ignored Hannah completely. She could not understand the guttural language of the Hessians, who were dressed in black. They went through the dining hall and made their way into the back rooms, which were not occupied at the moment. Then they went upstairs. From the piercing shriek that came from the big room, Hannah judged they had come upon Mr. and Mrs. Hewitt in their bed.

Hannah felt helpless. Was there nothing she could do? Suddenly she had an idea. She quickly made her way to the trap door that led to the cellar, opened it, and slipped down the steps. She bolted the cellar door from the inside, and went over to the ale casks lined up on shelves against the wall. "They'll at least not drink our ale!" she thought. She quickly turned on the spigot of each cask.

She could hear the men walking around in the dining room, their boot heels tapping on the wood floors. Now they were in the kitchen. What damage would they do? It would not make sense for them to wreck the place, reasoned Hannah. Presumably they wanted to stay here. The spigots of all the ale casks were opened now, their contents pouring out onto the dirt floor, which soon became a bog of mud. The air was heavy with the yeasty scent of ale.

Hannah took a deep breath, unbolted the cellar door, and started to push it open, but suddenly it was flung open, and someone grabbed hold of her arm.

"It's the little wench!" laughed the soldier, a big Hessian with slick, black hair and a thick German accent. "And she reeks of ale!"

Hannah shook her arm free of him. "Unhand me, Sir," she said, sticking up her chin and looking him straight in the eye. "My father is not here. You will have to leave."

The Hessian let out a roar of laughter. "Nay, that is not possible," he said. "We have already started to move in! Haw Haw Haw."

Hannah turned and saw Mrs. Hewitt with a bundle of bedding in her arms. "They took over the big room," she said, her voice quaking. "Just like they took over our home."

Hannah turned on her heel, picked up her skirts, and ran outside to tell Evie what had happened. "I am going to find Father!" she called.

She needed the fastest horse, so she led Badger out of the barn. He reared a little when she put the bit in his mouth. She would ride him bareback. There was no time for hoisting the saddle.

"Go inside and help Mrs. Hewitt," said Hannah. "Tell her I'll be back with Father and Thomas." Evie clenched her fingers together, making a stirrup, and gave Hannah a boost. Hannah gave Badger a nudge and turned his head toward the meadow. He reared again, so she dug in her knees and held on tightly. Soon they were galloping over the hill to the meadow's edge. Her mobcap blew off and her hair flew wildly as she rode to warn her father and Thomas.

Meanwhile, Evie quietly opened the door to the inn and went inside. From her corner by the hearth she saw the soldier –"lobster back" she'd heard them called – come reeling into the kitchen. He saw her too, her hands at her sides, fear in her eyes.

"You, wench!" he snarled. "Fetch me some ale."

"There is none, sir," Evie replied. The blow came so fast that Evie was stunned by its force and did not feel pain at first.

"How dare you address a soldier of the king thus!" he yelled, swinging his empty ale glass in the air. Evie stepped back, out of his way, and placed her palm over her cheek. When she pulled it away she saw that it was red with blood. She backed into the dining room. The door to the outside banged open and another soldier entered the room. This one was dressed in black and was swigging wine straight from the bottle. The wine he held must have come from Mr. Bedkin's cellar, for there was none at Hart's Tavern. Hannah had seen to that.

Suddenly the Redcoat turned away from the kitchen and faced the big Hessian. "Where did you get the wine?" he demanded. The Hessian took a pull from the bottle and wiped his mouth with the back of his hand.

"Wouldn't you like to know? He sneered. Then he lurched over to Evie and put his arm around her shoulders. He pulled her towards him with his free arm and took a swig from the bottle with his other. Evie struggled to pull away but could not break his grasp. Then the Redcoat intervened.

"Hands off, man," he shouted. "The wench is mine and she was about to fetch me some ale." He grabbed Evie by her arm and pulled her away from the Hessian, just as Mrs. Hewitt stomped into the room, hands on hips.

"What is going on here?" she demanded.

"Now, here's a fat wench for you!" said the Redcoat, pointing his chin toward Mrs. Hewitt and letting out a loud guffaw. This sent the Hessian into a rage. He tilted the bottle to finish the last drop of wine, and then smashed it over the back of a chair. He sent his fist into the face of the Redcoat, who responded by swinging wildly, upturning chairs and upsetting dishes and candles.

Evie watched in horror. She had not been abused nor seen such violence since the slave auction when she was a girl. Her heart pounded in fear, but also in anticipation. This was a turning point. She felt that things were about to change. This day was like the day the dam broke, and the river washed over its banks. Nothing would ever be the same after today, Evie was sure of it. Not even Peter Hart could fix this.

Then, as she looked around the room, she saw a ribbon of fire snake along the floorboards and up the corner of the dining room. What had started the fire? Was it a spark from the hearth? Was it a candle? No one ever found out for sure, and Evie did not care. She watched the flame with indifference, and the Redcoats and Hessians had yet to notice. She took her cloak from the peg and walked out the door.

She went to the barn, and stood there while Mr. and Mrs. Hewitt dragged out the hay wagon. "Grab hold and help us here, you fool!" yelled Mrs. Hewitt. But Evie did not move. She did not dare go back into the inn to fetch her few belongings. She simply wrapped her cloak around her as tightly as she could and headed for Camartha's cabin. Camartha would be able to contact Blanchard. Tonight, perhaps, they would be free.

By the time Hannah came back with Peter and Thomas flames were creeping along the edge of the wooden floors and up the walls. She ran to the stairway, screaming for everyone to get out of the inn. "Miss White! Miss White! She cried, as the fire crackled faster now, up the stairway towards the attic. The heat was becoming intense. Hannah ran outside then, knowing there was nothing more she could do.

Then she looked up in horror to see Miss White leaning out the little attic window. She was trapped! "Father, Thomas, she screamed. "We have to save Miss White! Suddenly Hannah saw Mr. and Mrs. Hewitt dragging the hay wagon from the barn. Thomas, Hannah and her father ran to the wagon and pushed it from behind until it was positioned under the window. "Jump, Miss White, jump!" screamed Hannah.

Looking from side to side, Violet crawled out of the window and on to the roof. There she hesitated for a moment before leaping and landing squarely in the hay wagon. For a moment she was stunned and breathless, as the wind was knocked out of her. But she was safe. In a few moments she stumbled to her feet and Peter Hart lifted her out of the wagon.

Thomas had started the bucket brigade. Mr. Bedkin and his slaves had seen the fire and had hurried to help, as did Polly Jewell and her sons, George and Jack.

The fire raged on, roaring like a furnace. Hannah could not believe what was happening. Flames shot out of the roof. The fire was more horrible than any hellfire Hannah had imagined during one of Reverend Windsor's sermons. She ran to the big oak tree where she had sat and rested on that warm and pleasant ale-making day. Now her father stood there with Thomas, watching the destruction. She coughed and coughed from the black smoke that permeated her lungs, trying to regain her strength so that she could help with the water buckets.

She made her way to the well, where she carried bucket after bucket to the men who stood in the brigade, pouring water on the fire. She knew in her heart that it was hopeless. They might just as well have been tossing thimblefuls of water. Yet she toiled on. She heard her father's shouts in the distance, giving instructions – making sure everyone had left the inn, and that no one would go back in for any reason. The animals had all been released from the barn and set loose.

The inn burned with a vengeance, as if giving up its life was preferable to submitting to the subjugation of the soldiers. At last, it succumbed to the flames. Then Hannah realized that everyone was accounted for except one person. Where was Evie? With a shock she realized that Evie could have been trapped. Hannah relived in her mind the picture of Miss White, standing in the window of the attic room, calling for help, then leaping from the roof into the wagon. Was Evie left behind?

No. Hannah suddenly remembered the image of Evie's frightened face by the barn, just minutes before the hay wagon had been pulled out to save Miss White. Hannah did not know Evie's whereabouts, but she prayed that she was safe.

# Chapter Thirty-one

Violet stood spellbound in the middle of the meadow, watching the black smoke rise from what was once Hart's Tavern. She put her scorched hand over her mouth, choking back sobs. Tears poured down her face. So much was had been lost since her arrival in New Kensington – her schoolhouse, Adeline's life, and now her friends' home. As she stood there alone, in her pale silk dress now torn and blackened with soot, she realized that she would leave New Kensington. She would go back to England, to Craven Street to live with her father, Catherine, and her little sister -- at least for a while. First she would travel to Salem, to the docks Thomas had told her about, where ships and commerce would abound after this God forsaken war. Violet looked up at the sky and saw that black clouds mingled with the smoke. Heavy drops of rain mixed with sleet started to fall. Violet picked up her filthy skirts and headed back to find Hannah. They would go to the only place she could think of – Goody Garlicke's cabin. There they would stay, with Wyanjoy and her baby. There Violet would rest and make her plans. There was nothing else to do.

That night, in the cramped space of Goody Garlicke's cabin, the voices of the women were quiet and somber. Wyanjoy's baby whimpered, eager to be nursed, oblivious of the disaster that had befallen the most recent arrivals to Goody's little house. Goody placed buckets of water over the fire so that the women could wash. She made herbal tea for them to drink, and applied poultices to their wounds. She gave them bread and butter and added water to the kettle of soup that hung over the fire to make it go farther. She took every last blanket and mat that she owned and placed them on the floor so the women could rest, and perhaps sleep, after the trauma they had been through. Hannah and Violet could say little, but feelings of gratitude were mixed with their pain, gratitude for Goody's care and for Wyanjoy, who stroked their arms and hands, and hummed a sad song as she wiped their faces with a cloth dipped in fragrant water.

Eventually Violet and Hannah fell asleep in front of the hearth. Neither was badly injured. Tomorrow would be a new day. Goody knew that the ladies of New Kensington, after hearing of the tragedy, would bring clothing and food, and take the women into their homes, finding room somehow among the quartered soldiers who had probably caused the fire. For tonight, they were safe here.

Goody went to the shelf near the door and took down her journal. Adjusting her new spectacles she could see clearly the words she had written in her spidery hand. She smiled to herself. What would her husband have thought of her, wearing spectacles invented by a famous man named Benjamin Franklin and sheltering three young women and a baby in their humble home? Wyanjoy continued her low singing as she nursed her baby. The song was familiar to Goody. She was sure that her husband had sung it to her long ago.

One never knows what life will bring, she thought. Perhaps she was meant to do this, to provide a way station for these women who had to stop on the way to their destinies. Goody felt a deep sense of satisfaction at that moment. She opened the door and looked up at the silver crescent of a new moon, showing itself between the clouds. The rain had stopped. She breathed the night air, which was tinged with the flavor of smoke.

Then she saw him – her mysterious rider in the distance. Only this time he was not alone. Leaning low and sitting behind him was someone else, a young woman whose skirts billowed behind her. She held the horseman tightly around his waist. Goody sensed there was a strong bond between the two – something about the way the horseman leaned into the wind, urging his horse to run faster than Goody had ever seen it run before. She knew at that moment it would be the last time she saw him. She closed the door and blew out her candle.

Just as Goody had predicted, the day after the fire the good women of New Kensington found places for Peter Hart's family in their homes. Hannah and Miss White were taken to Mrs. Braithwaite's house, where the parlor had been turned into a dormitory of sorts for the soldiers. Some of the quartered soldiers had to be displaced to make room, and thus slept in barns or the church. Hannah and Miss White took over Bea's bedroom, while Bea moved in with her mother.

"You are most kind," said Hannah to Mrs. Braithwaite and Bea.

"I hope you will be comfortable, my dears," she replied.

Peter Hart and Thomas went to stay with Polly Jewell, finding space with her sons, George and Jack. Miss Fisk, the postmistress, took in the Hewitts. All the other guests left for other inns. Evie was never seen again.

Later that day Hannah and her father made the sad journey from town to the charred remains of what had been their home. Her father put his arm around her. His other arm was around Polly. Hannah turned to him and tried to read what she saw in his face. She knew then that great change would happen, both in her own life and in the colonies. She saw her father with his arm tight around Polly's waist and knew at that moment that Polly Jewell and her father would work together to rebuild Hart's Tavern.

Hannah squeezed her father's hand and walked toward the barn, which was unscathed. The animals were safe. Then she saw something miraculous. On one of the beams near Honeycomb's stall was the small clay pot containing one of the little orange trees, one of the four Hannah had planted so many months ago.

Who had left it there? Evie? Miss White? Hannah would never know. She smiled to herself. The tree was alive. It had survived, just like her. Hannah decided at that moment that she wanted to live a life of adventure. She wanted to sail across the ocean and travel the world, to see exactly where these trees grew in the wild. She wanted to visit Miss White and her family on Craven Street in London, when this war ended. She wanted to go to Paris and learn French. Was this too much for an innkeeper's daughter to dream? No, decided Hannah. It was not.

For now, however, she would stay in New Kensington, until the inn was rebuilt. She was only fourteen years old, but in a few years she would go and live her own life. And one day, she was sure she would return to Hart's Tavern.

A few days after Hannah and Violet had moved into Mrs. Braithwaite's house, a wagon bumped along the cobbled stone road and stopped at the front door. In the back of the wagon was a large trunk, closed with leather straps. Under different circumstances, Hannah would have been curious about what was in the trunk. But today, as she stared out the window in idle boredom, she felt depressed and disinterested. There would be no more lessons, for Miss White would soon leave for England, as soon as she found passage on a ship out of Salem. What should she do? She wondered again and again.

Mrs. Braithwaite opened the front door and the driver pulled the trunk into the hall. Hannah could hear their voices, and then Mrs. Braithwaite's, calling her.

"Hannah! Someone has delivered something for you."

Hannah felt quite sure it must be a mistake. This was not her trunk. All her clothes and belongings had been destroyed in the fire.

She went downstairs into the hall where Bea and Mrs. Braithwaite were waiting. "Who sent this?" she asked. "Surely, it must be a mistake."

"Are you Miss Hannah Hart?" asked the driver.

"Yes, Sir, I am."

"Well, this trunk is for you. Mr. and Mrs. Squires sent it."

Hannah was speechless. Surely, they had not sent Adeline's trunk!

"Please take it to my room," she said, her voice quivering.

The man grumbled, but hoisted the trunk on his shoulder and carried it upstairs. Hannah felt for the coin in her pocket, which she would give to him for his trouble. She followed him to the small room she shared with Violet White, who was sitting at the desk.

Violet turned from her writing with a look of surprise.

"It is Adeline's trunk!" exclaimed Hannah, as she placed the coin in the driver's hand. "Mr. and Mrs. Squires sent it for me!"

Violet and Hannah knelt on the floor and undid the leather straps. Then, together, they opened the lid. Folded neatly inside were Adeline's clothes. One by one, Hannah and Violet removed the items. On top was Adeline's yellow silk dress and hair ribbon; then her rabbit fur hooded cloak and white kid gloves. Here were her leather boots, and pairs of heavy stockings. There were five every day dresses and two wool shawls of high quality. At the bottom were pages of music and a book of poetry – verses by Margaret Cavendish.

Hannah was reminded of the day she had opened her mother's trunk in the attic of the inn, and had taken out the petticoats for the secret signal. She remembered the blue dress, her mother's favorite. Everything had burned in the fire. She had nothing at all with which to remember her mother. Suddenly she started to cry. Violet held her in her arms as Hannah sobbed, for the loss of her mother, Adeline, and Hart's Tavern. Her shoulders shook as she wept as if her heart would break. Violet just held her and rocked her. When at last the storm subsided, Violet said softly, "We must try to think of the future. We can never go back to the past. It will always be a part of us, but we can never go back. Adeline would have wanted you to have these things. Some day you will wear them. Some day you will travel and learn and discover. You will live a life of adventure, I am sure of it."

# Chapter Thirty-Two

Goody stood with Wyanjoy and her baby, facing south. The sky was clear, the air was still. They could see the Great Bay, silver in the distance under a cloudless sky the color of azure. The two women said nothing, but they felt at peace with one another. Little Peter stirred and whimpered. Wyanjoy handed him to Goody, and he immediately snuggled down and quieted. The two women walked. They headed down the slope of the meadow to the place where the stone wall met the forest, where Evie had run to escape with Blanchard. They walked past the slave cabin of Mr. Bedkin where Camartha lived. They walked all the way to the spot where Hart's Tavern had stood. The barn was still there, but it was empty. The two women walked inside the barn to the spot where Wyanjoy had come that bitter December night, half frozen with her new baby. They stopped at the stall for a moment where Wyanjoy, Goody, and the child had spent the night. Silently, Wyanjoy moved close to Goody and placed a hand upon her shoulder. The gesture was one of gratitude, respect, and, above all, affection.

They women left the barn and headed toward the bay, to the path where the mysterious rider had galloped. Finally, Goody led Wyanjoy to the small rise the stood apart from the reeds, at the edge of the scrub pines, away from the beach. Here were the five smooth stones, the gravesite Wyanjoy had wondered about. Finally Goody spoke. "Here lies my husband. He was one of your people. Goody set Peter down on the grass. Wyanjoy said nothing, but bent down and laid both her hands upon the stones, as if somehow she could communicate with the ghost of the man who was buried there. "He was a good man, and I loved him," said Goody. Her voice was calm and even. "We wanted a child. I'd like to think that somehow little Peter is a part of him, that I can have a place in his life. That I was meant to find you that night."

Wyanjoy stood up and faced Goody. She took both of her hands and said,

"My friend, Good Woman. You will be a grandmother to my son." At that moment a breeze stirred in the air and the tall grass swayed in the wind. Goody put her finger to her lips and bent down to touch the stones. Then slowly, she stood up. Wyanjoy held Little Peter in her arms, and the two women went home.

The End

# Notes

While the story of Hart's Tavern is a work of fiction, many of the historical events mentioned actually took place, and some of the characters mentioned in the story are real, or based upon actual people.

The first chapter of the book in which Hannah Hart is confronted by the Redcoats and dyes the bread blue is based upon an actual event described in *From Sketches from Local History,* by William Donaldson Halsey. Phebe Squires and her husband Ellis of Squiretown, Long Island, tried to hide their herds of livestock and other property from the British. Halsey describes how Phebe saved her bread by dipping her flour into a dye pot.

The character Goody Garlicke is based upon the only person arrested for practicing witchcraft on Long Island. In *From Sketches from Local History,* Halsey writes that Goodwife Garlicke was arrested for practicing witchcraft in East Hampton. She had many influential friends, among them Col. Lion Gardiner, who presented such a strong defense at her trial that she was acquitted. Halsey writes, *At the trial it was proved that she had used herbs to bewitch with, and that she had no objection to being thought a witch.*

Benjamin Franklin mentions the Native American Wyanjoy in his writings, Vol. IV: *Sally, whose Indian name was Wyanjoy, a Woman much esteemed by all that knew her, for her prudent and good Behaviour in some very trying situations of Life. She was a truly good and an amiable Woman .*

William Floyd left his Mastic Beach estate for Philadelphia after signing the Declaration of Independence. Before the British troops moved into Long Island, his family fled to Middletown, Connecticut. Soon after, his estate in Mastic was occupied by British troops.

The story of an Indian giving birth in the snow and being rescued in a wagon was inspired by an anecdote in Halsey's book about a Shinnecock Indian who became stranded in a snowstorm with her twin babies. Halsey writes,

*She walked across the Hills toward home carrying her babies, facing the storm and struggling against the tempest until very tired and exhausted, when she decided she could never reach home in such a blinding snowstorm . . . she wrapped her babies in blankets in the basket . . . and placed them in the lee of a cedar tree . . . and started for the nearest help; this proved to be a farmhouse west of the village of Southampton. It was then late in the night. She told the man her trouble and where she had placed her babies. Without hesitation he yoked inns oxen on the cart and with her started to the rescue.*

In his book *Woman's Life in Colonial Days,* Carl Holliday writes of women carrying their spinning wheels through town enroute to a meeting of the Daughters of Liberty. He writes,

*It became a matter of genuine pride to many a Patriotic dame that she could thus use the spinning wheel in behalf of her country. Daughters of Liberty, having agreed to drink no tea and to wear no garments of foreign make, had spinning circles similar to the quilting bees of later days, and it was no uncommon sight between 1770 and 1785 to see groups of women, carrying spinning wheels through the streets, going to such assemblies.*

The British occupation and billeting of troops on Long Island took place from the Washington's defeat in the Battle of Long Island on August 27, 1776 until Evacuation Day on November 25, 1783. Their 2,653 day occupation was a time of hardship for the colonists. Historian Silas Wood, who lived through the occupation as a child in Huntington, Long Island, wrote,

*The whole country within the British lines was subject to martial law, the administration of justice was suspended, the army was sanctuary for crimes and robbery. The officers seized and occupied the best rooms in the houses of the inhabitants. They compelled them to*

*furnish blankets and fuel for the soldiers, and hay and grain for their horses. They pressed their horses and wagons for the use of the army. They took away their sheep and cattle, sheep, hogs and poultry, and seized without ceremony, and without any compensation, or for such only as they chose to make for their own use, whatever they desired to gratify their wants or wishes.*

The scene in which Hannah tries to hold the British soldiers and Hessians at bay with her father's rifle was inspired by the story of a 60-year-old widow named Hannah H. Brown, recorded in *From Sketches from Local History,* by William Donaldson Halsey. He writes,

*It was in the Autumn of 1777, on a pleasant evening, that a file of armed soldiers, without ceremony entered the house of Mrs. Brown and ordered her to open the door of the room containing the liquor, or they would stave it down. At this threat, she rushed between them and the door, against which she placed her back. The enraged officer swore her instant destruction, and with great violence thrust the muzzle of his gun against the door on one side and then on the other of her person, just as near as he could without hitting her. She stood facing and thus addressed him. "You unfeeling wretch, you hired tool of a tyrant, your conduct is worse than a savage. I am without a human protector, but you know, Mr. Officer, surrounded as you are with men and arms, that I despise your threats, and if you pass the threshold of this door, you will first pass over my lifeless body." Such emphatic language from a lone woman, at such a time and place was too much for his cowardly soul to withstand. He grumbled but made a hasty retreat. The woman died in the Autumn of 1789, aged more than eighty years.*

The scene where Hannah goes to the cellar to open all the beer kegs so that the British could not drink it was inspired by Halsey's account of Elizabeth (Betsey) Glover who was the wife of Tavern keeper Jeremy Vail. In September 1781, the British burned New London Connecticut and then massacred the garrison at Fort Griswold at Groton. From there they passed over the Sound to Orient Point, Long Island. Jeremy saw the soldiers coming up the road. Elizabeth knew there were only two hogs-heads of cider left in the tavern. She went alone to the cellar, knocked out the bungs of those hogs-heads containing the liquor so that the cider would all run out, and then ascended the stairs just in time to meet the ruthless gang, who were *besmeared with the blood of her murdered countrymen at Groton. They flourished their swords and swore vengeance on the American rebels.*

Evie's search for the cake baker who might help locate her siblings is based upon a cake baker who was a freed slave in New York City who helped to raise children of all races. The individual is documented by the New York Historical Society.